"You're going to have to make up your mind."

Mark put out a hand, turning Nora to face him. "I told you I wouldn't pressure you," he said softly. "I'm a patient man, but I have my limits."

"Mark, I value your friendship so much—" she began.

"That's not what I want," he broke in impatiently. "It's got to be one way or the other."

Nora's mind raced. She dreaded the thought of giving him up entirely, but she simply didn't love him in the way he wanted—the way he deserved— to be loved.

"Are you giving me an ultimatum, Mark?" she asked at last.

He looked at her thoughtfully. "I guess maybe I am."

Rosemary Hammond lives on the West Coast, but has traveled extensively with her husband throughout the United States, Mexico and Canada. She loves to write and has been fascinated by the mechanics of fiction ever since her college days. She reads extensively, enjoying everything from Victorian novels to mysteries, spy stories and, of course, romances.

Books by Rosemary Hammond

Don't miss any of our special offers. Write to us at the following address for information on our newest releases.

Harlequin Reader Service
P.O. Box 1397, Buffalo, NY 14240
Canadian address: P.O. Box 603,
Fort Erie, Ont. L2A 5X3

THE WRONG KIND OF MAN

Rosemary Hammond

Harlequin Books

TORONTO • NEW YORK • LONDON
AMSTERDAM • PARIS • SYDNEY • HAMBURG
STOCKHOLM • ATHENS • TOKYO • MILAN
MADRID • WARSAW • BUDAPEST • AUCKLAND

Original hardcover edition published in 1990
by Mills & Boon Limited

ISBN 0-373-03193-9

Harlequin Romance first edition May 1992

THE WRONG KIND OF MAN

CHAPTER ONE

NORA stared down at the open file on her desk and tried one more time to concentrate on the columns of figures. She'd already sharpened her pencils twice, mopped up the cup of coffee she'd spilled and taken yet another trip to the Ladies down the hall to wash her face with cold water—her fourth time that morning.

The minute she tried to focus on the rows of meaningless numbers they began to swim before her eyes, and the same thing happened again. The normal, everyday office noises, the telephones ringing, typewriters clacking, the low hum of voices that drifted into her small cubby-hole, gradually became muted until they faded away completely, and she was trapped once again in the prison of her own dull misery.

She squeezed her eyes shut hoping to blot out the awful memories, without noticeable success, and when she opened them again a tear dropped down on the corporate tax return she'd been battling with all morning. She reached into her jacket pocket, took out a tissue and blew her nose. It was no use. This meant another trip to the Ladies.

She had just pushed her chair back and risen wearily to her feet when a small redhead burst into the tiny room.

'I think I'll go to lunch now, Nora,' she said. 'Can you take care of——?' She stopped short and stared.

'Sure, Jackie,' Nora replied, struggling hard to smile. 'You go on. What do you need me to do?'

Jackie took one look at her, then walked slowly towards her and put a hand on her arm. 'Listen, Nora, why don't you go home?'

Nora shook her head vigorously. 'I can't. I have too much work to do.' She gestured distractedly towards her desk, which was piled high with manila file folders. 'If I don't plough my way through the rest of these tax returns soon, the Internal Revenue Service is going to decide they can do without my services.'

Jackie gave her a long, appraising look. 'Don't you think you might feel better if you talked about it?' she asked softly. 'I mean, I know you like to keep your personal life to yourself, but we've worked together for dear old Uncle Sam for two years now, and I thought we were pretty good friends.'

'I can't, Jackie,' Nora replied in a tight voice. 'If I talk about it, I'll really go to pieces.'

Jackie thought a moment, then wheeled around and marched back to the door. She shut it firmly, came back to Nora's desk and sat down in her chair. 'All right,' she said. 'Go to pieces. Who cares?' She eyed Nora carefully. 'It's got to be a man. I know you've been seeing someone. What happened? Did he call it off?'

Nora shook her head. 'No. I did.'

'Well, you must have had a reason. What was it? Was he gay? An alcoholic? On drugs? A criminal? An international spy?'

Nora only stood there shaking her head. After a time, as Jackie's suggestions became more and more outrageous, she was almost smiling. 'My, you have a vivid imagination,' she commented at last.

Jackie threw up her hands. 'Well, what was it, then?' she exclaimed. 'Was he married?'

Nora's face immediately began to crumple. She turned her head away as the tears welled up once again. When she finally had herself under control, she turned back to face her friend. 'Can you believe it?' she asked.

'Well, I'm trying,' Jackie remarked drily. 'But it's not easy. You, of all people. That's the last thing I would have expected. When did you find out?'

'A few weeks ago.' Nora gave herself a little shake, and sighed. 'No, that's not quite true. I think I'd suspected it for a long time. You know how it goes. He didn't live here in Washington. He always stayed in a hotel when he was in town. We met in out-of-the-way places. He never talked about his home or his friends.'

'Who is the rat?' Jackie asked.

Nora waved a hand in the air. 'That's not important now. There's no point in spreading gossip about him. He has an important post on a senior senator's staff. He also has three children. I might be tempted to murder him, but I could never bring myself to harm his family. It wouldn't change anything.'

Jackie got up from the chair. 'Well, kiddo, I'm sorry. The same thing happened to me once, before

I married Bill. I don't know what it is with these goofballs that they think they can get away with that kind of thing.'

'Probably because we let them,' Nora commented wryly. 'I should have confronted him weeks ago with my suspicions.'

'How did you find out?'

'He left his wallet at my place one night. I couldn't stop myself from going through it. You know how it is when you're in love, especially when you already have doubts. There was a picture of him with his wife and children, and when I asked him about it later he caved in right away.'

'Well, I'm sorry, Nora. I mean it. You're certainly not the kind to get involved with a married man, so don't kick yourself too hard. You may have had your suspicions, but love is blind. I don't blame you for trying to close your mind to them. You wait and see. One of these days a nice *single* guy will come along.'

Nora shook her head. 'I don't think so, Jackie. I always seem to fall for the wrong kind of man, and after this experience I don't think I'll ever trust myself again. What's a single woman to do? Ask every man she meets for a sworn statement that he isn't married before she'll even go to dinner with him?'

Jackie glanced at her watch. 'Listen, I'm supposed to meet Bill for lunch at twelve-thirty, but I can cancel it if you need me to stay.'

'No. You go ahead. I'll be all right. There's never much business during the noon hour. Maybe I can get some work done.'

'Well, I'd better get going then. We can talk more this afternoon.' She gave Nora's arm a little pat and headed for the door.

'Thanks, Jackie,' Nora called after her. 'You were right—I do feel better.'

Jackie turned around and gave her a little salute. 'What else are friends for?'

When she was gone, Nora sat back down at her desk and tackled her figures once again. The department of the Internal Revenue Service that she and Jackie worked for had to do with audits of corporate tax returns. Their jobs were to go over any that were particularly large, looking for questionable deductions. If they spotted any, they would recommend an audit of the filer's books, a procedure that was never looked on with favour by the taxpayer.

Even though she did feel much better after her talk with Jackie, she still couldn't work up much interest in this one. She made a quick trip down the hall to the Ladies to wash her face and repair her make-up, for the last time, she hoped, and when she was through she gazed in the mirror at her reflection.

It wasn't so bad. Even though her heart was broken, and she felt so crushed inwardly, her appearance hadn't really changed. Somehow she'd expected to look as terrible as she felt, but her short, smooth black hair shone with life and health, her colour was good—at least, better than it had been a few days ago—and her trim figure still fitted well in the red woollen suit, even though she'd been certain she'd lost at least ten pounds through her ordeal.

She started back towards her own office, hoping she might be able to get some work done now. It was the lunch hour, and the large outer room where the clerical staff worked had emptied out completely, so at least it would be quiet. She was just about to turn into her room when she heard the main door open and close, footsteps coming towards the front counter, and a man's voice calling to her in a loud, commanding tone.

'Excuse me.' It was more a bark than a request. She turned around. 'Yes?'

'I want to see——' he reached into his jacket pocket, took out a piece of paper and consulted it '—a Miss Nora Chambers.'

She threaded her way around the desks and went up to the counter. 'I'm Nora Chambers.'

He slammed the paper down on top of the counter. 'Well, maybe you can explain this to me,' he growled angrily.

His hostile tone put her immediately on guard, and as she reached for the paper she gave him a quick look. She was all alone in the office, and their branch of the IRS had to handle some pretty irate customers. Although his face was flushed, at first glance he didn't appear particularly threatening. He was dressed conservatively in a dark suit, white shirt and plain dark tie and was carrying a good leather briefcase. His dark hair was well-cut, his face clean-shaven.

But he was a very big man, heavily muscled under the well-tailored jacket, with wide shoulders, a massive chest, large, callused hands, and he seemed very angry indeed. He was breathing hard, his big chest heaving under the crisp shirt, his eyes were narrowed at her, and there was a belligerent curl to his wide, thin mouth.

'Go ahead,' he snarled. 'Read it.'

She glanced through it. It was addressed to a Mr Mark Leighton, and was a standard letter that was sent to large taxpayers whenever there seemed to be discrepancies in their returns, and merely asked for clarification of certain items before determining whether an audit was necessary.

'Yes,' she said when she was through. 'What seems to be the problem?'

He leaned over the counter and pointed a finger at her. 'The problem,' he enunciated in hard, clear tones, 'is that you people are calling me a liar.'

'It's merely a standard form, Mr Leighton,' she explained calmly. 'It doesn't mean we don't believe you, only that we have certain questions that need to be answered in more detail.'

'You're threatening me with an audit!' he exclaimed loudly.

'Not threatening, only warning,' she said in a reasonable tone of voice.

'What's the difference?'

'The difference is that we need to have you explain a few things before we decide whether to go ahead with an audit. If you'll just respond to our questions, preferably in writing, I'm sure we'll be able to straighten it out.'

He lifted up his briefcase and slammed it down so hard on top of the counter that Nora almost jumped out of her skin. Still red-faced and glowering, he snapped it open, drew out a crumpled sheaf of papers and shoved them at her.

'I've written letters!' he shouted. 'And all the answers I got back were written in government gobbledegook. I've tried to explain on the telephone, but only got a run-around. I finally decided to come in person, and if it takes me all day, so help me, I'm going to get this thing settled once and for all.'

Nora knew when she was beaten. He meant it. 'All right, Mr Leighton,' she said. 'Why don't you come into my office? I'll get out your file and take a look at it.'

He only nodded curtly, snapped the briefcase shut and stomped heavily over to the gate. Nora unlatched it and ushered him inside. He followed her wordlessly to her office, planted himself on the one visitor's chair and folded his arms across his chest, while Nora went to the filing cabinet against the wall.

When she found the Leighton folder, she sat down at her desk and opened it. She'd been so distraught for the past few weeks with her own personal problems that she'd felt lucky to make it in to work at all, much less pay close attention to her caseload. As she glanced through the file, however, the details came back to her.

Mark Leighton owned a large farm in Virginia, just over the border from Washington DC. He raised thoroughbred horses and had several acres of cherry and apple orchard. He employed twenty people full-time, fifty more during harvest season. His tax returns, she noticed, were prepared and signed by Anthony Leighton, a lawyer.

When she was through, she looked across the desk at him and gave him her most patient, placating smile. 'Well, Mr Leighton, I think we can work this out to our mutual satisfaction. Apparently, there is some question about your deductions for farm equipment. Since your major source of income is from horse-breeding, we felt that perhaps you were claiming too much for the orchard crops. Now, all we need is a more detailed breakdown of——'

'I don't have time for that,' he stated in a flat tone. 'This is one of the busiest times of year at my place.'

Although his voice was even and controlled, his jaw was set in a hard line, and his face seemed to be getting redder by the minute. Obviously he was not going to co-operate or give an inch, and her patient explanations might as well be given to the wind for all the impression they made on him.

'Mr Leighton, there isn't anything I can do unless you give me the figures I need. There are certain regulations, guidelines I have to follow in order to do my job. Can't you understand that?'

Nora heard her voice shake on the last few words. She was finding it harder and harder to maintain her composure. Although she was certain by now that the man was harmless and had no intention of doing her bodily injury, her nerves, shaky enough to begin with even before this man had shown up, were about to give way. She could already feel the hot tears prick behind her eyes.

He leaned forward and slammed the palm of his hand down hard on top of her desk. 'Now, you listen to me,' he snarled in a low, menacing tone. 'I've been paying taxes for my place, on time and perfectly honestly, for fifteen years, and I'll be damned if I'm going to——'

Suddenly Nora couldn't endure another minute of Mark Leighton and his mulish persistence. She leapt to her feet, and in one wide, sweeping gesture sent the entire contents of the file off her desk and on to the floor. 'Oh, all right!' she cried. 'Have it your way. I don't even *care* about your problem, Mr Leighton.' Then the dam broke and she burst into tears.

She covered her face with her hands and stumbled blindly past her desk, heading towards the door. Her one instinct was to run. But when she reached it she came up against a solid, immovable object.

She dropped her hands and raised her head to find herself gazing directly at Mark Leighton's broad chest. Her eyes flicked upwards. He was looking down at her, his face drained of colour, with an expression of utter horror.

'Lord, I'm sorry,' he muttered hoarsely. He raised a hand, but when she flinched back from it he instantly let it fall to his side. 'Listen, I didn't mean to——'

'Oh, never mind!' she groaned. 'It's not you. Please just get out of my way and let me pass.'

'But it is me,' he said, still blocking her path. 'I feel responsible. See, I've got this temper, and while I manage to keep it under control most of the time, dealing with the IRS can be so frustrating that I——'

'I don't *care* about your problems, Mr Leighton!' she cried. 'Can't you understand?' Still he didn't budge. 'Listen,' she went on, 'I sympathise with you, I really do. But right now I've got problems of my own.'

He continued to gaze down at her, his broad face set in a grave, speculative expression, one heavy dark eyebrow raised. Then, after a few moments of this careful scrutiny, he asked abruptly, 'When was the last time you ate?'

She stared up at him open-mouthed. 'What's that got to do with it?' she asked.

He smiled suddenly, and chuckled deep in his throat. The smile utterly transformed him. His eyes were a soft, deep brown, kind eyes, crinkled at the corners, and were looking at her now with real concern. He put one of his big hands lightly on her arm and shrugged diffidently.

'I'm a farmer. We believe that the cure for any ailment is food. Have you had lunch?'

Wordlessly she shook her head.

'Then let me buy you some.' He stepped out of her path, but kept a firm grip on her arm. 'Come on. You wait and see. You'll feel better when you've had something to eat.'

Nora was so stunned by his sudden about-face that her tears were forgotten. 'I don't even know you,' she said.

'Sure you do.' He tossed his head in the direction of his file, still lying on the floor. 'Everything you need to know is right in there. Please come. I lost my temper over something that wasn't your fault, and I want to make it up to you.'

Suddenly Nora realised she really was hungry, starving even, for the first time in days. In spite of their inauspicious beginning there was an air about Mark Leighton that she found reassuring, something like an older brother or a caring friend. She couldn't quite put her finger on it, but it had to do with the fact that there wasn't a hint of sexuality in his manner towards her. He seemed to be interested in her as a person, not a potential bedmate, and actually to care about her distress.

'All right,' she said at last. 'We really should discuss your tax problem anyway, and we might as well do it over lunch.'

He nodded, and they went out into the main room, which by now was gradually filling up with Nora's co-workers, who had started drifting back from lunch. When they reached the gate at the front counter, Jackie was just coming through.

'I'm going to lunch now, Jackie,' Nora said, stepping aside to let her pass. 'Mr Leighton has come in from Virginia to discuss his tax situation. I won't be long.'

'Sure,' Jackie said in a somewhat bewildered tone. 'No hurry. I'll see you later.'

Nora could feel her friend's eyes fastened firmly on her back as she and Mark Leighton made their way towards the glass door at the front entrance. She had to smile. If she knew Jackie, her friend was already dreaming up a new romance for her. She'd explain later.

It was a brisk autumn day with a slight nip in the air, and out on the street the usual throng of tourists visiting the nation's capital clogged the pavements, even though it was late September now and the school year had already started in most states.

Since it was past one o'clock, the restaurants in the area would already be fairly empty of the office workers that swarmed into them during the noon hour, and they would have a wide choice of places to eat.

As they approached the entrance of a good Italian restaurant just a few blocks away from the office, Nora turned to her companion.

'Do you like Italian food?'

'Yes, very much.'

'Let's give it a try, then.'

He held the door open for her and they stepped inside, to be greeted by a strong aroma of garlic and rich tomato sauce. While they waited to be seated, Nora turned to him.

'You live with your mother?' she asked.

'Well, she lives with me is probably a better way of phrasing it,' he said. 'We're a rather old-fashioned bunch, and, since it's a family farm with a big house, we naturally all live together.'

The plump Italian hostess came bustling over to greet them just then and they followed her to a quiet table at the back of the dining-room. When they were seated, she handed them menus and asked if they cared for a drink before lunch.

Nora shook her head. 'Not for me, thanks. I have to stay alert this afternoon.'

'I'll have a glass of your house red,' Mark said.

When the hostess was gone, Nora leaned back in her chair and eyed the man across from her. He seemed quite relaxed, his elbows resting on the table, as he consulted the large menu.

'What did you mean,' she asked, 'when you said you all lived together?'

'Well, there's my mother and father, my older sister, Anna, and younger brother, Anthony. As I said, it's a family business.'

'Anthony,' she said. 'He was the one who prepared your tax return, wasn't he?'

'Yes. He's the bright boy of the family. A lawyer *and* an accountant. He's also much more qualified to deal with the IRS than I am, but he's off on a business trip at the moment, and I had to do something about you people or explode.'

Nora winced. 'All right. As long as we're here, let's try to come to some kind of solution about that tax return. Maybe we can compromise.'

For the next hour they discussed the fine points of Mark's tax situation while they ate. By the time they finished lunch, they had arrived at a mutually satisfactory understanding. It was after two o'clock, and time for Nora to get back to work.

Mark asked for the bill, and after he had paid the hostess they went back out on to the street, walking along together in companionable silence. Nora's spirits had revived considerably after the wonderful meal, and she was relieved to get at least one of her clients' tax problems resolved.

When they reached her building, she turned to him to say goodbye. 'Thanks very much for the lunch,' she said. 'You were right. I do feel better.' She held out a hand. 'And I'm glad we got your taxes sorted out.'

He took her hand. 'Thanks for the company,' he replied with a smile. 'I enjoyed it.'

'Goodbye, then,' she said.

She started to pull her hand away from his, but when he didn't release it she gave him a puzzled look. He was frowning down at her, apparently deep in thought and not really seeing her. Then, as though making up his mind, he nodded and let her hand go.

'Nora,' he blurted. 'Have dinner with me tonight.'

Nora hesitated. She liked the man, felt comfortable with him, had even come to respect his honesty and integrity, but she simply wasn't attracted to him, and it wouldn't be fair to him to let him think she was.

'Mark,' she said slowly, 'I don't think that would be such a good idea.' She paused, wondering how much to tell him. 'You see,' she went on at last. 'I'm just coming out of a relationship that went sour, and I don't want to even consider another involvement right now.' She laughed. 'Or possibly ever again, for that matter.'

He lifted his broad shoulders in a shrug and smiled at her. 'Listen, I only asked you to have dinner with me, not elope.'

Nora's face went up in flame. 'I'm sorry,' she muttered. 'I just wanted to make sure you knew how I felt.'

'That's OK. There are no strings. I like you, Nora, like being with you. I'll be leaving tomorrow, in any case, and I'm rather at a loose end tonight. That's all there is to it.'

'Well, all right,' she said slowly.

'Good. Shall I drop by here at quitting-time?'

'You might as well. I'll be working late anyway, trying to catch up on about a hundred things that should have been done weeks ago. Say, six-thirty?'

'All right. I'll be here.'

Still he made no move to leave. They continued to stand there in front of the building, with the traffic noises in the background and other pedestrians skirting around them. He was eyeing her carefully, a thoughtful frown clouding his face, and seemed to have something on his mind.

'Well,' Nora said at last. 'I guess I'd better get inside. We seem to be blocking traffic.'

He reached out a hand as though to stop her, without quite touching her, then nodded brusquely and dropped it to his side. 'I'll see you at six-thirty,' he said.

Then, abruptly, he turned from her and walked away. Puzzled, Nora looked after him, half expecting him to come back, but in a few moments he had disappeared into the stream of pedestrians. Whatever he'd had on his mind, he'd obviously decided to let it go. She pushed the glass door open and walked inside.

As she made her way through the busy outer room back to her own office, she began to wonder if she'd made a mistake in agreeing to go out to dinner with him. That last look on his face still bothered her. Although he seemed to accept her condition that there was to be no emotional involvement, she'd learned the hard way that quite often what a man said and what he meant were two entirely different things.

Well, it was his look-out, wasn't it? She'd warned him. If he had something else in mind besides a dinner, it wasn't her problem. Actually, the very fact that she wasn't attracted to him was what made it safe for her to accept the invitation in the first place.

When she reached her office she saw Jackie standing by the open door, obviously waiting for her, a frankly inquisitive look on her sharp little face. She followed Nora inside, shut the door behind her and stood there, her arms folded across her chest.

'Well,' she said. 'What was that all about?'

'I told you,' Nora replied. 'He came all the way in from his place in Virginia to discuss his tax problem.'

'Since when does dealing with irate taxpayers include having lunch with them?'

Nora stooped down to pick up the file she had swept to the floor earlier and started putting it back in order. 'Well, there was a little more to it than that,' she explained as she worked. 'He came storming in here after you left, breathing fire and ready to do battle over the letter I'd sent him weeks ago asking for a clarification of his deductions. He was fed up with the run-around he thought he'd been getting, and decided to come in person. He was *very* upset. I finally got him calmed down, and since neither of us had eaten he offered to buy me lunch.'

'And that's all?'

'Jackie, what more could there be?'

'And you're not going to see him again?' Before Nora could reply, Jackie had tossed her red curls in disgust and was shaking a finger at her. 'You really take the cake, Nora. Here's a man who is obviously interested in you——'

'Oh, come on. How do you know that?'

Jackie raised her eyebrows. 'I can just tell, that's all. He had that hungry look about him.'

Nora shook her head firmly. 'You're wrong. He didn't make one move or give me one sign that he was interested in anything but his taxes. Besides, I'm through with all that. I've been burned for the last time. Never again.'

Jackie sighed. 'Well, I still think this Leighton guy looks promising, and with a little encouragement...' Suddenly she clapped her hand over her mouth and smothered a shriek of dismay. 'Don't tell me,' she intoned in a sepulchral voice. 'He's married.'

Nora laughed. 'No. In fact, he lives with his family. Mother, father, brother and sister.'

'Well,' Jackie breathed, visibly impressed. 'You can't get much more respectable than that. He looks prosperous, too.'

'Respectability and prosperity have nothing to do with it!' Nora was beginning to lose patience with her importunate friend. 'I'm not interested in romance, and even if I were, it wouldn't be with Mark Leighton.'

Jackie's eyebrows shot up. 'Why on earth not? He's a darned good-looking man.'

Nora looked up from the file. 'Oh, do you think so?'

'Don't you?'

Nora shrugged. 'Oh, I guess. He's not my type, though.'

Jackie snorted. 'Huh! A fat lot of good your "type" has done you in the past.'

'Jackie, I have work to do,' Nora said in a warning tone. 'A *lot* of work.'

'OK, OK. I'm leaving. I'll mind my own business from now on, but——'

'Out!' Nora interrupted, pointing at the door.

Jackie grinned, gave Nora a mock curtsy, and scurried out of the door. When she was gone, Nora finished straightening out Mark Leighton's file, glancing over the returns as she did so. Meeting the man in person somehow made the figures more meaningful, and she soon saw that Jackie was right. He was indeed a prosperous man. The farm he owned with his family paid off handsomely.

Why couldn't she fall in love with a man like that? She tried to picture him again in her mind. It wasn't that he was ugly, or repulsive, or even particularly unattractive. In fact, Jackie was right, he was a good-looking man, with his dark colouring and muscular build, his well-fitting clothes and air of assurance.

But she'd really meant it when she'd told Jackie he wasn't her type. Her taste had always run to slight, slim men, fair men with blond hair and blue eyes. Clever, complex and sophisticated men who were usually over-achievers. Not only were Mark Leighton's looks all wrong, but he was clearly a simple, direct man who said only what he thought, seemed perfectly content with his life, and apparently didn't intend to make any demands on her.

In fact, he was about as far from Stephen Kincaid in every respect as it was possible for a man to get, which by rights should be a major plus in his favour. If she had any sense, she'd at least try to work up an interest in him.

She gave herself a little shake and set the Leighton file aside. At least they'd straightened out his tax situation, and that was one problem taken care of. She'd go out to dinner with him tonight, he'd go back to Virginia, and they'd never see each other again. That was how it would work out, how it should be. He might be prosperous and eligible, but it would be wrong to give him any encouragement when she was so convinced it couldn't possibly go anywhere.

With a sigh, she reached for the next file from the tall stack on her desk and opened it.

CHAPTER TWO

THAT evening Nora and Mark went back to the same Italian restaurant where they'd had lunch. Not only was it conveniently close by, but by the end of the day Nora was so tired after the busy afternoon she'd put in trying to catch up on neglected work that she didn't feel like exerting the necessary thought and energy to come up with somewhere new.

An even more cogent reason, however, was that the closer it came to six-thirty, the hour they had agreed to meet, the more she regretted having made the dinner date with him in the first place. What she wanted to do was go right home, heat a can of soup and curl up in front of the television set where she wouldn't have to think. Now she was committed to having dinner with this stranger. Her only hope was that he had either forgotten about the date or decided she wasn't worth bothering about, and stand her up.

But when she emerged, the last one to leave at that hour, there he was waiting for her outside the building. When she saw him her heart sank. She couldn't go through with it. But, on closer inspection, he looked so harmless and inoffensive standing there, calm and relaxed, his hands in his trouser pockets, she decided it couldn't possibly hurt her just to have one dinner with the man.

The moment he caught sight of her his eyes lit up, and he came walking towards her, smiling broadly. 'You're right on time,' he remarked as she fell into step beside him. 'Amazing.'

'Oh, I'm a working girl,' she commented lightly. 'I'm used to meeting deadlines.'

He had no objection to going back to the same restaurant when she suggested it, and they walked the short distance in companionable silence. It was an early dusk, and the street-lights were already lit. The sky had clouded over during the afternoon, and, although it was still warm, there was a hint of rain in the air.

The restaurant was more crowded this evening than it had been at lunchtime, and the hostess informed them they'd have to wait in the bar for a table.

Mark gave Nora an enquiring look. 'How about it? Would you like a drink?'

'Sure. I might as well, since I don't have to go back to work.'

There was plenty of room in the bar, and they sat down at a small corner table. The room was dim, with only a flickering candle set in the centre of each table, and, except for the clink of glasses, the low murmur of conversation and muted music playing in the background, very quiet.

Nora ordered a vodka gimlet, and Mark decided to stick with wine. When their drinks arrived, he raised his glass briefly in the air and took a healthy swallow.

'Well,' Nora said, 'while I was slaving away for Uncle Sam, what did you do with your afternoon?'

'You'll laugh,' he said.

'No, I won't.'

'Well, then, I did some sightseeing. Took in the Lincoln Memorial, climbed up the Washington Monument. I even stood and gawped at the White House, hoping for a glimpse of the President—or at least his dog.'

She laughed.

'Hey,' he said, hurt. 'You promised you wouldn't.'

'I can't help it. If your home is in Virginia, which can't be more than a few hours' drive, how come you've never taken the Cook's tour of the capital before now?'

'Well, we're pretty busy down on the farm,' he said with a fake nasal twang to his voice. 'But as a matter of fact I have toured Washington, many times. I just never seem to get tired of it. I find it inspiring to connect with the country's roots once every so often.'

'Ah,' she said. 'A patriot.'

He shrugged. 'I suppose so. Pretty old-fashioned, huh?'

'No. I think it's nice. Having grown up here, I tend to forget what it all means, our history, how our government works.'

By the time they finished their drinks, the hostess appeared and led them to a table in the dining-room. They ordered dinner, and while they waited for it Mark continued his running commentary on the afternoon's activities. Nora tried to work up enough interest to at least pay attention, but she only half heard what he was saying and soon found her mind wandering.

Whether it was the gimlet she'd downed so hurriedly, or the work she'd put in that afternoon, or merely her general depleted state of mind, she couldn't tell, but her head began to feel heavier and her spirits more lethargic by the minute. Her eyes began to glaze over, and she recognised all the signs of the all too familiar load of depression that was quickly descending on her.

Suddenly she realised he'd asked her a question. She started, gave him an apologetic look and said, 'I'm sorry. What did you say?'

He eyed her speculatively for a moment, took a sip of wine, then blurted out, 'Have you been sick?'

She stared at him. 'No. Why do you ask?'

'Your mind was a million miles away.' He shrugged. 'I have to admit that a rundown of the sights isn't my idea of sparkling conversation either, and I can understand how it might put you to sleep. But you look positively ill, and I was just wondering why.' He hesitated. 'It must be the guy.'

'What guy?' she asked guardedly.

'Well, you mentioned at lunch that you'd just come out of a bad relationship.'

She lowered her eyes to her plate and began to push her Veal Florentine around with her fork. 'Well, yes,' she mumbled. She looked up at him. 'But that's all over. I've put it behind me.'

He raised a heavy dark eyebrow. 'Oh? Are you sure?'

Nora felt her face flush. 'Well, I'm trying hard.'

'Listen, I know it's none of my business, and I certainly don't mean to pry into your affairs.' He hesitated once again, then leaned forward and gave her a direct look. 'But for the life of me I can't imagine how the hell any man could hurt a woman like you badly enough to put that look on your face.'

Nora was just about to make a tart reply, agreeing with him that it was none of his business, when all of a sudden it dawned on her that actually he was paying her a sincere compliment, and she had to smile. 'Now, what makes you say that? You don't even know me.'

He had finished his dinner and set his napkin down beside his plate. He raised the wine bottle and gave her an enquiring look. When she shook her head, he emptied the remains into his own glass, leaned back in his chair and took a long swallow. Then, still holding the empty glass between his long fingers, he put his elbows on the table and gazed intently at her through half-closed eyes.

'You're right,' he said in a low voice. 'I don't really know you. But I'd like to.' He set the glass down and laced his fingers under his chin. 'I'll tell you what. We spent lunch talking about me and my family. Why don't you tell me about yourself?'

'What do you want to know?'

He grinned broadly. 'Well, for one thing, how did a nice girl like you get into a dirty business like tax-collecting?'

She laughed. 'Well, believe it or not, I was good at maths when I was at school and just drifted into working for the IRS, mainly I suppose because nothing better came along. I'm rather a passive type, I guess.'

'That surprises me. I took you for a dedicated career woman.'

She thought a minute. 'I did start out that way. You know, I wasn't going to get stuck taking care of babies or slaving in the kitchen waiting on some man while he went out and did all the interesting things.'

'Ouch!' he said with a pained look.

She smiled. 'Sorry about that. I was only trying to explain that at that particular time in my life marriage and a family didn't appeal to me.'

'And now?' he asked in a casual tone.

She shrugged. 'Now I'm not so sure. It seems that what starts out as interesting work always becomes dull routine after a while. There are times I think I made a mistake in choosing a career over marriage.'

'It's not too late, you know.' He cocked his head to one side and gave her a long, appraising look. 'Let's see. I'd say, according to your biological clock, it couldn't be more than six or six-thirty at the latest.'

'If you're asking me how old I am, I'm twenty-seven.'

'Well, then, you've got lots of time. Maybe the right man just hasn't come along yet.'

She gave him a glum look. 'That could be my problem. I thought he did. More than once, as a matter of fact.'

He raised an eyebrow. 'You do have a problem, then?'

'It looks that way,' she said wryly.

'The man you mentioned today,' he began cautiously. 'Is he part of it?'

She gave a harsh laugh. 'He's *all* of it.' She eyed him suspiciously. How had he got her talking like this about her personal affairs, something she rarely did with even her closest friends?

As though sensing her unease, he immediately changed the subject. 'How about your family?' he asked. 'You said you grew up in Washington. You must be close to them.'

'Not really. I'm an only child, so no brothers or sisters. My father was a civil servant, worked for the department of the Interior. He took an early retirement, and he and my mother are now on a world cruise. They sold the house before they left, and, from what I can see, intend to spend the rest of their lives travelling.'

Just then she heard a slight commotion behind her, a woman's voice raised, calling Mark's name. He shifted his gaze, looking past Nora, a sudden frown darkening his face. It was gone as quickly as it had appeared, and he started to rise out of his chair.

Nora turned her head around to see a tall blonde walking towards their table. When she reached it, she gave Nora a quick glance and turned to Mark, who was on his feet by now.

'Mark Leighton!' she cried. 'Of all people!' She threw her arms around him and kissed him full on the mouth. Then, still gripping him firmly by the forearms, she pulled back and gazed up at him. 'What in the world are you doing here? I thought you never left the farm.'

'Hello, Sylvia,' Mark said with a tight smile. 'I had some business to take care of.' He gently disengaged himself and turned to Nora. 'This is Sylvia Armstrong, a neighbour of mine. Sylvia, Nora Chambers.'

After the two women had exchanged brief, polite greetings, Sylvia turned all her attention back to Mark. As they chatted, Nora watched them. The message had been unmistakable, as such messages are between two women, that the blonde was staking her claim on the tall dark man and wanted Nora to understand that fact.

If she only knew, Nora thought with wry amusement, how little she has to fear from me. She was quite a good-looking woman, about Nora's age, with that aristocratic, well-bred, outdoors look that some country women had. She was deeply tanned, her hair bleached to a pale gold from the sun. She had on only a hint of make-up and wore her expensive black suit like a model for a sleek magazine.

'Won't you join us for an after-dinner drink?' Mark was asking her now.

'No, thanks. I have a party waiting for me. We're going on to a club for dancing. Will you come along?' She turned to Nora and gave her a sweet smile. 'And Miss Chambers, of course.'

Nora hastily gathered up her jacket and handbag and jumped to her feet. 'No, I'm sorry, I can't. Thanks anyway, but I really should get home. You go ahead, Mark. I'll take a cab.'

'Oh, yes,' Sylvia said, obviously delighted. 'Do come, Mark.'

'No,' he said firmly. 'I wouldn't hear of it. I'm going to see Nora home.'

Nora laughed. 'Mark, I find my way home from this part of town every night of the week. There's no need for you to...'

But he had already turned away and was saying goodbye to the crestfallen blonde, who was trying to pin him down now to joining her party after he took Nora home. As far as Nora could tell, he didn't agree to anything one way or the other.

'It was nice to meet you, Nora,' the blonde said as she turned to go. Their eyes met, and once again the message came across loud and clear: he's mine. Keep off. For one wild moment Nora had the impulse to make an announcement out loud right then and there that she had no designs whatsoever on Mark Leighton, but by then Sylvia had walked away.

'Do you really have to go home?' Mark asked her.

Nora glanced at her watch. 'Well, I am rather tired.'

He nodded and raised a hand to a passing waiter for the bill. After he'd paid, they went outside and walked the few blocks to the car park where he'd left his car, a foreign model that Nora was unfamiliar with but which looked expensive. She'd never owned a car and knew nothing about them. They got inside and Nora gave him the directions to her apartment.

'Your friend Sylvia is certainly a lovely-looking woman,' she remarked after they'd driven along in silence for a while. 'I take it there's some kind of understanding between you.'

His head swivelled around abruptly, and he gave her a brief glance. 'No,' he said shortly. 'We're just old friends.'

That's what *you* think, Nora mused to herself. Then, aloud, she said, 'I think you're missing a

good bet there. Sounds as though you have a lot
in common. Don't you want to marry?'

'I suppose I do,' he replied in a slow, thoughtful
tone. 'I've been so busy with the farm that I haven't
had much time for romance.' He laughed shortly.
'My brother, Tony, takes care of that sort of thing
in our family.'

'I see. I take it he's married, then?'

Mark shook his head decisively. 'Oh, no. Nothing
like that. He's five years younger than I am, thirty-
two, and claims he's too young to settle down. What
I meant is that he's the one who seems to attract
women like bees to honey. You'd have to meet him
to understand what I mean.' He gave her another
quick, sideways glance. 'In any case, there's nothing
between Sylvia and me.'

'That may be true,' Nora said cautiously, 'but I
certainly got the impression that, with any encouragement from you, she'd be interested in something more than friendship.'

'I doubt it,' he said in a rather terse, distant tone.
'Sylvia just likes to play games.'

They had reached her apartment house by now,
and Mark pulled into a vacant spot at the kerb. 'I'll
see you to the door,' he said when he'd switched
off the engine.

Before she could tell him that really wasn't necessary, he was out of the car and had come around
to open her door for her. For such a big man, he
moved quite swiftly. She stepped out on to the
pavement and, as they walked towards the entrance, she got her key out of her bag. At the door
she turned to him.

'Thanks very much for the dinner, Mark. And I'm glad we got your taxes taken care of.'

He grinned down at her. 'And you won't send me any more threatening letters?'

She laughed as she stuck her key into the lock and turned it. 'No. I promise. You're all clear with Internal Revenue.' She pushed the door open and stepped inside the lobby.

'That's a relief,' he said. 'Thanks for your help, and thanks especially for your company tonight.'

'Goodnight, then,' she said.

He seemed about to say something more to her, but, if so, he obviously changed his mind. He only said a brief goodnight, turned from her and walked away towards the car.

Nora closed the door and walked up the one flight to her own apartment. She hadn't been fibbing when she'd told him in the restaurant that she was tired. It was a much healthier kind of fatigue, however, than she'd experienced for weeks. This came from hard work rather than the anguish of a broken heart.

It had been good for her to get out, too. Mark Leighton was pleasant company. She felt relaxed around him. He was so easy to talk to. Maybe it was possible after all for men and women to be friends without the burden of romantic involvement. Too bad she'd never see him again. She would have liked to be friends with such a man. It wasn't on the cards, however. Not only was he tied to his farm, but she couldn't imagine the lovely Sylvia tolerating Mark's friendship with any other woman, however innocent.

*   *   *

Although in the days that followed thoughts of Mark Leighton gradually faded from Nora's mind, she realised that on some level that odd encounter with him marked a turning-point for her, even that in some way he was responsible for her improved outlook on life in general.

For one thing, her work gradually improved, both her efficiency and her interest in it. She *was* good at figures. It was a kind of language to her. She felt at home in the world of numbers, had a talent for dealing with them, and was once again grateful for the good job that allowed her to use that talent.

Although she began to feel more sociable, she remained adamant on the subject of men, turning down one invitation after another from well-meaning friends who wanted her to meet their recently divorced male relatives, and consciously avoiding making eye contact or using any of the unconscious body language that signalled interest with the men she did meet on the job or at parties.

It was at a dinner party given by an old schoolmate of hers that she saw Stephen again. She'd had to work late and was the last one to arrive. There were at least twenty people present, and they were just finishing their cocktails before going in to dinner when she showed up, breathless from the rush, full of apologies for her hostess.

'I'm really sorry to be so late, Liz,' she explained as she shed her coat. 'I hope you weren't waiting for me.'

'Not at all,' her friend replied, taking her arm and leading her towards the others. 'I think you know just about everybody here.'

They made a quick circuit of the room. Nora stopped to greet those she knew, and Liz introduced her briefly to the others. They had come to the last cluster of people standing just at the entrance to the dining-room when she spotted him, the fair head, the graceful, slim carriage, the elegant clothes. She stopped dead in her tracks.

Liz stared at her. 'Is something wrong?'

Nora recovered her composure enough to give her a quick, apologetic smile. 'No, I just caught my heel in the carpet.'

They continued on their way, and as they approached the fair man he raised his eyes. They widened slightly when he saw Nora, and she put on a deliberately bland expression. There was no avoiding it. She'd have to speak to him. She only prayed she wouldn't be seated next to him at dinner.

'Here's someone I bet you haven't met,' Liz was saying as she drew her forward. 'This is Stephen Kincaid, Senator Fallon's top aide, and his wife Ginny.'

Nora gave Stephen a blank look and a cool smile. Their eyes met and held for a second, and to her horror she could feel the old insidious tug of longing rising up in her once again. She had loved this man, believed he'd loved her. Now here he was, standing before her, his wife at his side.

'How do you do?' she murmured, as Liz pronounced her name to the Kincaids.

She tore her eyes away from Stephen and turned to look at his wife. She was a small brunette, as dark as Stephen was fair, as dark as Nora herself, and Nora mused wryly that at least his taste ran true to form. They chatted for a few moments about neutral topics, and then Liz announced dinner.

Somehow Nora got through the rest of the evening without making a fool of herself. Although she was painfully conscious of Stephen's attempts to catch her eye on several occasions, she studiously avoided both Kincaids throughout the long, excruciating dinner, where thankfully they sat nowhere near each other.

As soon as they rose from the table when the meal was ended, Nora grasped the first opportunity she could to draw Liz aside and, pleading a headache, managed to make her escape without having to speak to him again.

In the taxi driving back to her own apartment, Nora sat rigid on the back seat, her hands clenched into fists, tears smarting behind her eyes, and regarded herself with utter loathing. She was still attracted to the man! No matter how badly he had treated her, no matter how she despised him, she couldn't hide from the fact that he could still arouse a spark of desire in her.

That unsettling episode only confirmed her vow of celibacy. Falling in love was too risky. She simply couldn't trust herself. While she would never have dreamed of entering a relationship with Stephen if she'd known he was married when they'd first met, she'd still learned the hard way that her judgement about men was terrible.

Something had to be seriously out of kilter in her basic make-up, in her very genes. Perhaps it was her metabolism. Whatever it was, it clearly meant one thing: *all* men were out, for good.

* * *

Soon it was the middle of October, and the days were getting cooler, the nights positively frosty. Nora always enjoyed the autumn weather, and was looking forward to a cosy winter with hot cocoa before a wood fire, lots of good books she'd been meaning to read—and no men.

One Friday afternoon just before home-time, she was finishing off a long, involved case she'd been working on when Jackie came into her office. Nora glanced up at her, flipped the file closed, leaned back and stretched widely.

'It's almost five o'clock,' Jackie said. 'Are you about ready to leave? Bill said he'd pick us up in front of the building on his way home from work.'

Nora gave her a blank look. 'Am I missing something here?' she asked at last.

Jackie put her hands on her hips and narrowed her eyes. 'Don't tell me you've forgotten. You agreed two weeks ago to come to dinner at our place tonight and help me decide on the new curtains for the bedroom I'm redecorating.'

Then the light dawned. 'Oh,' Nora said in dismay. 'That's right, I guess I did.' She rose from her chair. 'I don't suppose you feel like letting me beg off. Honestly, when it comes to decorating I'm the last person to give you advice. You've seen my apartment. My mother says she's certain I'm colour-blind.'

'Nora, you promised,' Jackie said sternly.

Nora heaved a sigh. 'Oh, all right. Don't get excited. I'll come. It's just that I think you could do a lot better if it's decorating advice you want.'

Nora got up to go and get her coat, and it wasn't until she was putting it on that she realised something didn't quite ring true. She turned and looked at Jackie. 'It's a man, isn't it?' she said accusingly.

Jackie raised innocent eyes. 'What makes you think that?'

'The truth, Jackie.'

'Oh, all right. But it won't hurt you to come anyway.'

'Jackie, how many times have I told you I wasn't interested in blind dates?'

'About a hundred,' Jackie said with a grin. 'But listen, Nora, I went to a lot of trouble to get Tom for you. He's a prime catch, a flaming heterosexual, and he is *not* married, at least at the moment. He's also just your type—you know, sensitive.'

'Hah!' Nora said. 'That's all I need—another sensitive man.'

'Well,' Jackie spluttered, 'if you won't do it for me, you could at least have the decency to consider poor Tom's feelings.'

'Tom's feelings are not my problem,' Nora retorted. 'You invited him. You consider his feelings. Besides, since women outnumber men by about two to one in this town, he won't have any trouble finding someone to repair his ego.'

It was a week before Jackie would even speak to her, but finally one morning just before noon she came into Nora's office and, after a shaky start, she managed to get out a brusque apology, admitting she'd been the one in the wrong.

'OK,' Nora said. 'Let's just forget it.'

'I still think you could have——'

'Jackie,' Nora said in a warning tone. 'I mean it.'

'All right. I know when I'm beaten. But just tell me this. Is it your intention to spend the rest of your life alone?'

'Yes.'

Jackie goggled at her. 'You're not serious.'

'But I am. Listen, it's not such a great tragedy. I'll get a cat, or maybe a bird.'

Jackie shook her head slowly from side to side. 'I don't believe you, Nora. You've got everything going for you: brains, looks, personality. And now, just because of one mistake, you've decided to live like a nun the rest of your life.'

'In your catalogue of my qualities, you left out the most important one,' Nora commented drily. 'Bad judgement.'

Jackie threw her hands up in the air. 'All right!' she exclaimed. 'I give up.'

'I hope you mean that.'

Jackie gave her an odd look. 'I guess I really do mean it this time,' she said slowly. 'I'm sorry for you, Nora. I hope you change your mind one day.'

'Not a chance.'

'Well, anyway, we're still friends, aren't we?'

'Of course. Still friends.'

Once it actually penetrated Jackie's stubborn head that Nora really wasn't in the market for romance, it wasn't long before Nora's other friends got the message, too, and the offers gradually stopped coming. Soon the invitations did, too, and Nora found herself with an awful lot of free time hanging heavily on her hands.

It seemed that people weren't that interested in going out of their way socially for a single woman, especially one who avoided male company, even for an evening. Nora didn't blame them—she probably would have felt the same way. But no matter how lonely she got, or how empty her evenings and weekends seemed, she was never once tempted to go back on her vow. It was just part of the price she had to pay for her congenital bad judgement.

She thought vaguely that she might take an evening course at the nearby college, perhaps learn a foreign language. She could travel. Learn how to play the piano. Go to concerts and movies and shows on her own or with her single women friends.

The trouble was, she wasn't really passionately interested in any of these things, and most of the women she knew were either married or so busy looking for eligible men that they really couldn't be bothered doing the things Nora might enjoy.

So the weeks dragged on in a kind of emotional limbo. She went to work every day, usually had lunch with Jackie, came home to an empty apartment, ate a solitary dinner standing at the kitchen counter, and, after reading the newspaper and watching a little television, went to bed early. Weekends she spent cleaning her already spotless apartment, shopping, and doing laundry.

Occasionally it would occur to her that it wasn't much of a life. Even her job had become dull routine, once she'd recovered from Stephen and got on top of it again. Still, it was a safe life, far, far preferable to the turmoil created by the men *she* always managed to fall for, and, while she wasn't thrilled with it, neither was she miserable.

One Friday night in late November, the telephone rang just as she stepped inside her apartment. When she answered it, a man's voice came on the line.

'Nora? Nora Chambers?'

'Yes, this is she.'

'This is Mark Leighton. Remember me?'

For a few moments, Nora couldn't place him. It had been at least two months since she'd seen him, and then it had only been briefly. Once she connected the man with the voice, however, she remembered what pleasant company he had been that day, and was quite pleased to hear from him again.

'Of course I do,' she said quickly. She laughed. 'I just wish all my irate taxpayers were so agreeable.'

'Glad to oblige. I just wish all civil servants were so interested in their customers' problems.'

'What are you doing back in the big city? I thought you never left your farm.'

'I had some business to take care of in town this afternoon and decided I might as well stay the night.'

'Don't tell me you're going to do more sightseeing.'

He chuckled. 'I might at that,' he replied. 'What I'd really like is to see you. Are you free for dinner tonight?'

'Yes, as a matter of fact I am.'

'Shall I pick you up in an hour or two? Say, seven-thirty?'

'That sounds fine. I'll be ready.'

CHAPTER THREE

IT WASN'T until they'd ordered dinner and were drinking their cocktails that Nora began to doubt the wisdom of accepting Mark's unexpected invitation. At the time, she hadn't thought twice about it. Somehow, she didn't connect this kind, thoughtful man with romantic problems at all. Going out with him had seemed no more threatening to her than having dinner with Jackie, or perhaps the older brother she'd never had.

Since then, however, she'd noticed some familiar signs. He was as courteous and attentive as ever, quite relaxed, chatting casually about his horses and orchards, his family, but there was a definite difference in his manner tonight, and it bothered her. As he spoke, she watched him carefully, trying to pin down the nature of that difference.

The way he was looking at her, for one thing, the expression on his face, just a suggestion of a more than friendly interest in his dark brown eyes. She'd dressed casually in a soft woollen dress, a luscious shade of cherry-red, that was in no way suggestive but which did mould the soft curves of her body. The light in his eyes when he'd first seen her that evening had been unmistakable, and his hands had lingered on her shoulders just a little too long when he'd helped her on with her coat.

The wine steward came up to the table just then for their order, and while the two men discussed it

Nora gave Mark a closer look. He didn't *seem* to have anything else on his mind except choosing wine. As she watched him, there suddenly popped into her mind the comments Jackie had made about him that first day he'd come storming into the office.

How had she put it? She'd said he was a good-looking man. Prosperous. Respectable. He was all of those things, and, from the looks he'd been getting from a party of women at a nearby table, Jackie wasn't alone in her assessment. Then there was Sylvia, who obviously would kill to get him.

He was turned in profile to her, his head raised to speak to the *sommelier*. There was no question. While he was not film-star handsome, there was something about the way his strong features were put together that any woman would have found attractive. She noticed for the first time that there were flecks of grey in his black hair near the temples.

He dressed conservatively, and, while there was no flair or fashionable style in his dark suit, muted tie and white shirt, his clothes were obviously expensive and hung well on his muscular frame. His hands were large, the palms callused—a working man's hands, but clean and well-cared for.

In addition, unlike the men she'd been involved with in the past, he seemed totally unaware of his good looks. His air of quiet confidence and authority was simply a natural expression of the inner man, not some act he was putting on to impress her.

She must be out of her mind! Any normal woman would jump at the chance to attract a man like

Mark Leighton, and here she was worried about how to discourage him from getting amorous ideas about her. What was wrong with her, that she could be so conscious of all his fine qualities and still feel not the slightest twinge of desire? But just let some slick loser come along, and she'd be putty in his hands.

She looked away, biting her lip so hard in sheer self-disgust that she drew blood. Sunk in her glum reverie, she didn't realise he was speaking to her until she heard him call her name, so sharply that she half jumped out of her chair.

The wine steward had left, and Mark was staring at her with a puzzled look on his face.

'I'm sorry,' she said. 'I'm afraid I was woolgathering. What did you say?'

'I was asking how things stood with you and the man you were involved with the last time we met.'

She made a face. The question only escalated her sense of danger, deepening the sinking feeling she already sensed that what had promised to be a pleasant and rewarding evening would turn into a battle of wills on the way home.

'That's all over,' she said in a rather curt tone. 'It was over even then.'

As though sensing her reluctance to discuss her personal affairs, he changed the subject immediately. 'How's the job going?' he asked lightly. 'Have you had to do battle with any more angry citizens?'

'Oh, yes,' she replied, relieved. 'That's the name of the game in my business.'

He finished off his martini in one last swallow. 'What are your prospects there? You must have expectations for advancement.'

'That all depends on what's available. Civil service is rather a strange little world. First there has to be a position open, then you have to pass an examination to be placed on a list, and if you qualify you *might* get the job. There are so many regulations now that give various minorities precedence that it's very "iffy".'

'Well, presuming everything went smoothly, what would be the next step up for you?'

She thought a minute. 'I guess that would be director of our particular office.' She smiled. 'You know, the one that writes those letters threatening an audit.'

'But from the way you've described how it works, I take it you'll have to wait until it's available.'

She nodded. 'Actually, that position should come open quite soon. Our current director is retiring in January. I've taken the test, passed it and been placed high on the list, so I have a pretty fair shot at it.'

They continued to discuss neutral subjects throughout the dinner, and gradually Nora's reservations about the situation faded. When they were finished eating, the waiter came to clear away their plates and asked them if they'd like an after-dinner drink.

Mark glanced at her. 'How about it, Nora? Anything for you?'

'No, thanks. I've already had enough to drink for one evening with cocktails and wine.'

'That'll be all, then,' he said to the waiter. 'I'd like the check now.'

When the bill had been paid and they'd gone out to the car, Mark turned to her before starting the engine. 'It's still early. Is there anything else you'd like to do? A movie? A club?' He laughed. 'I'm not much of a dancer, but I'd be willing to give it a try if you like.'

'I don't think so, Mark,' she replied. 'It's been a long week for me, and I'd just as soon turn in early.'

He didn't say anything, but from the look on his face she could tell he was disappointed. To pass the awkward moment, she twisted around to adjust her seatbelt. When she turned back to him, he still hadn't started the car. His hands were in his lap, and he was staring down at them intently.

Finally, he raised his head and turned to give her a direct look. 'What's wrong, Nora?' he asked quietly.

'Nothing. I just think I'd better go home.'

'Something's bothering you,' he stated flatly.

She was about to tell him a polite fib, perhaps manufacture a headache, but then decided against it. If she couldn't be honest with a man like Mark Leighton, she really was in pretty bad shape. He was so forthright and direct himself that he deserved better.

'All right,' she said. 'I guess there is.'

'Are you going to tell me about it?' He smiled. 'Somehow I have the feeling I'm the cause of it, at least partly.'

Suddenly she knew it would be all right. Given her past experience with men, it was difficult to comprehend, but apparently he really didn't intend to make any demands or create a scene. He seemed to be sincerely interested in what was troubling her.

'When we met two months ago,' she began in a careful voice, 'I tried to make it as clear as possible that I wasn't interested in anything beyond friendship. You seemed to accept that.' She paused to examine his reaction.

He nodded. 'That's right.'

'Well, it could just be my imagination, but from the signals I've been getting from you tonight it seemed to me you might have forgotten.'

'No,' he said quietly. 'I haven't forgotten.'

'Then it *is* just my imagination,' she said with undisguised relief. 'I was wrong.'

He stared down at his hands again for a few moments, then raised his eyes to her. 'You weren't wrong. I just didn't think I was that obvious.'

'You're not,' she said with a smile. 'I'm just rather paranoid on the subject. My antenna picks those signals up by remote control.' She took a deep breath. 'Without being offensive, what I'm trying to say is that I haven't changed my mind. I still feel the same way about getting involved.'

He smiled crookedly at her. 'I guess I was hoping you had changed. It's why I asked you at dinner about the other man.'

'It isn't you,' she said bleakly. 'It's me.'

'The guy that did this to you,' he said softly. 'He must be some prize.'

She waved a hand in the air. 'Oh, the problem isn't only with him. I have a long, colourful history of choosing the wrong man. Don't misunder-stand,' she added hastily. 'I'm not saying that I've had one full-blown affair after another— I mean, actual *affair*, if you know what I mean. Thank heaven I've had more sense than that. But when I fall, I fall hard, and it's always ended in disaster.'

'In what way?' he asked.

She gave a dry, harsh laugh and began to tick off on her fingers. 'Well, this last one was married, and I didn't know it. The one before that turned out to be a drunk. A *mean* drunk. Then, let's see, there was one who couldn't hold down a job, and another who vowed undying love for me and about six other women all at the same time.' She sighed. 'There were others, not quite so devastating, but I don't really need to go on, do I?'

'So you've got it all figured out that every man you meet is going to let you down, deceive you in some way, make you suffer.'

'No, of course not. Just the ones I fall for. That's why I decided I wouldn't even date any more.'

Before the words were out of her mouth, she realised what they implied and how it must sound to him. The message was clear. She *had* accepted his dinner invitation. She gave him a wary look, all primed to soothe a ruffled ego.

To her amazement, he threw his head back and burst out laughing. She could only goggle at him. Every man she'd ever known would have given her a hurt look and fallen into a sulk until she'd ended up apologising, just for telling the truth.

'Well,' he said at last. 'At least we know where we stand.'

She squirmed uncomfortably in her seat. 'Mark, I didn't mean to hurt your feelings.'

He widened his eyes at her. 'Listen, I won't pretend I'm not disappointed, but believe me, the truth is more important than my feelings.' He leaned closer to her. 'I like you, Nora, I really do. And I'd like to see you again, as often as you'll let me. No strings, no demands.'

She shook her head sadly. 'I don't know, Mark. I just don't think it's such a good idea.'

'You don't have to give me an answer now,' he said quietly. 'Look at it this way. Since you're not attracted to me, I don't present a threat of any kind to you, and there's no danger. So why refuse to see me again?'

'It's not myself I'm worried about. That kind of arrangement is hardly fair to you.'

'You let me worry about that,' he stated firmly. 'You've been honest with me. I can't ask fairer than that, and I certainly have no right to ask for what you can't give.'

She frowned. 'I still don't think——'

'Listen,' he broke in. 'I already told you. I like your company. We can be friends, can't we?' He grinned. 'Besides, who knows? In time you might change your mind.'

She still wasn't sure. She liked him a lot, she respected him, enjoyed being with him. But how long would that satisfy him? Sooner or later he'd try again. But before she could think of a good answer, he had started driving off.

When they reached her apartment, he walked with her to the entrance. At the door he gave her a polite handshake, and thanked her for the pleasant evening. Then suddenly, with no warning, he put his hands on her shoulders, leaned down and kissed her lightly on the mouth. His mouth felt warm and dry on hers, very nice, in fact, and she was too startled to protest anyway.

After a few moments he pulled his head back, gave her shoulders a squeeze and grinned down at her. 'Friends kiss,' he announced defensively.

She had to smile. 'All right,' she said in a grudging tone. 'Just don't push me.'

He raised both hands in the air. 'Never!' he declared stoutly. 'Listen,' he said just before he turned to go. 'I don't know when I'll get back to Washington, but I'll call you when I do. You can count on that.'

Then he was gone.

Later that night, as she was getting ready for bed, she mulled over the events of the evening, and finally came to two conclusions: that she had acted honourably in telling him the truth about how she felt, and that he had taken it very well—so well, in fact, that she decided he had to be a man without very strong passions.

He'd said he'd call her again the next time he came to town, but somehow she doubted it. It was too bad. He was a nice man, head and shoulders above most of the men she knew. He was also far from stupid and must realise there was no future in it.

Christmas came and went, and soon it was January. There had been one heavy snowfall on New Year's Day, and the temperature had remained below freezing ever since.

By now the long evenings reading by the fire and drinking cups of cocoa had begun to pall. Each morning Nora pulled on her heavy boots, thick woollen jacket, gloves, scarf and hat and crunched her way to the bus-stop to stand there shivering with the other commuters waiting for the bus that was always late.

That meant she either had to stay an hour extra at night, getting home long after dark, or spend her lunch hour working at her desk to make up her time. It had begun to seem as though she spent her entire life in the dark. A bright, crisp autumn was one thing; these short days of deepest winter quite another.

She had virtually no social life to speak of. Her women friends all seemed to be either hibernating or in love. And the job she used to enjoy had become eight long daily hours of excruciating boredom. She hadn't heard from Mark Leighton again, nor did she expect to after what had happened the last time she'd seen him.

There was one bright spot in this bleak perspective. The director of her department had finally retired. The whole office was agog, on pins and needles, waiting for the final word from on high about his successor.

One Friday afternoon, Nora and Jackie had braved the slick, icy streets and biting wind off the Potomac River to dash out to a nearby fast-food restaurant for a bowl of hot soup. They sat side by side at the counter, discussing the situation.

'By rights you should get it,' Jackie said between spoonfuls. 'Not only do you have seniority over the rest of us, but you were placed higher on the list.'

'I don't know, Jackie. The civil service seems to have a strange set of rules. At least, I've never understood them.'

'I think they make them up as they go along,' Jackie muttered glumly. 'But I still think you'll get it.'

'Maybe. But I'm not counting on it. They could always bring in someone from outside. And don't forget the handicapped and minorities have an edge.'

Jackie shrugged. 'Well, I guess that's fair enough, but for this particular job I doubt if those rules will apply. I mean, after all, the director of a department is a pretty high-level position. I think they'll decide this one on merit alone.'

Nora finished the last drop of soup and pushed her bowl away. 'I hope you're right. I could use a bright spot in my life right about now.'

Jackie shot her a swift look. 'Is something wrong?'

Nora made a face then forced out a dry laugh. 'Oh, just life in general. I think I've got the winter blues.'

'Huh! I know what's wrong with you.' Jackie scraped the bottom of her bowl. 'You need a man in your life.'

Nora rolled her eyes heavenward. 'Oh, please, spare me. We've been all over that a hundred times before.'

'Sure. Pardon me. I forgot—you know best. That's why you're feeling so wonderful.'

'And a man would solve everything. Is that it?'

'Well, it couldn't hurt to try.'

'I *have* tried, Jackie. Lord, how I've tried! What do you want me to do? End up with another loser?'

Jackie spun around and fixed her with a stern look. 'Every man is not a loser, my girl,' she stated firmly. 'Just because you've made a few mistakes in the past doesn't mean you should give them up forever.' She cocked her head to one side. 'What about this Mark Leighton? He seems like a nice guy.'

'I told you. He's not my type.'

'As far as I'm concerned, that's a major plus in his favour,' Jackie retorted.

'You could be right. It doesn't matter. Last time I saw him I made it pretty clear that I wasn't interested in getting involved, and I haven't heard from him since.'

'Why don't you call him?'

'And tell him what?'

'Tell him you'd like to see him again.'

'Then he'd think I was interested in him romantically, and I'm not. He just doesn't turn me on.'

Jackie shook her head. 'You're hopeless. Come on, we'd better get back to the grind. Maybe there'll be some word about the new director.'

That night, after dinner, Nora had just settled down in front of the television when the doorbell rang. She jumped half off the couch, startled, then rose slowly to her feet and walked over to the door.

She put a hand on the knob. 'Who is it?' she called.

There was a short silence. Then a man's low voice. 'It's Stephen, Nora. Can I come in?'

Her mouth dropped open. Stephen! What in the world could he want? She hadn't even thought about Stephen Kincaid, the most recent man to break her heart, for months, not since the time she'd run into him at that party, back in November, with his wife.

She glanced at her watch. It was almost ten o'clock. 'What do you want, Stephen?' she asked at last.

'I just want to talk to you,' he replied in an urgent tone.

Nora made a face. That was just like Stephen. *He* wanted to talk. It was always what *he* needed, never mind what suited her. She had half a mind to refuse, but her curiosity was aroused by now.

She undid the chain bolt and opened the door. He was standing there, one arm stretched out, his hand propped against the wall, leaning forward as though he might fall on his face any moment. He looked terrible, his pale blue eyes bloodshot, dark circles under them, his suit wrinkled, and he needed a shave.

'What is it, Stephen?' she said irritably.

He gave her a pathetic, hangdog look. 'I need to talk to you. Can I come in?'

'Oh, all right,' she said with a sigh. She opened the door wider. 'But make it quick. It's getting late.'

Once inside, his old air of confidence seemed to return. He straightened up and gazed around the room. The television set was still on, now showing a commercial.

'Do you suppose I could have a drink?' he asked.

'No,' she snapped. 'You know I hardly drink at all, and I don't keep anything but sherry in the house.'

'Sherry would be great,' he said hopefully.

She pointed to the sideboard where a bottle of sherry and several glasses were set on a tray. 'Help yourself.'

He went over to the sideboard, poured himself a glass and drank it down in one gulp. Then he poured another, and came back to her. He stood there for a moment, sipping the sherry this time, and eyeing her carefully.

'You look great, Nora,' he said at last. 'You've gained a little weight.'

She folded her arms in front of her and glared at him. 'Just tell me what you want, Stephen, and then go.'

He downed the last of the sherry in his glass and gave her a direct look. 'I've left my wife,' he stated bluntly.

Nora stared at him. 'You've done what?'

He went back to the sideboard, set the empty glass down, then turned to face her. 'You heard me.'

He began to walk slowly towards her, stopping just inches away. He raised a hand as though to touch her, but when she shrank back he dropped it to his side. He sighed dramatically.

'I know you have every reason to hate me, Nora, after the way I treated you, lied to you, deceived you. But all along it was you I really wanted. I see that now. I can't tell you how I've missed you, wanted you. Now that I'm free, we can be together again.'

Nora was so dumbstruck that when he reached out for her again she could only stand there, rooted to the spot. He moved in closer. She could smell the sherry on his breath, feel his arms snake around her, see his face coming closer, and still she couldn't move.

Her head was whirling. She couldn't think. She knew he was going to kiss her, and she still couldn't budge. She had loved this man once, desired him above all others. Now she hated him. Didn't she? His hold on her had tightened, pressing her against him, his hand moving up and down her back in slow, sensuous strokes.

Insidiously, she felt the heat rising within her. Stephen had always made her react that way. She couldn't fight him then, and she couldn't fight him now. She closed her eyes, waiting.

Then his mouth came down on hers in a wet, open-mouthed kiss, and as his tongue pushed against her lips Nora could feel herself beginning to respond. But suddenly, out of the blue, an image leapt into her mind, a man's face. Mark Leighton's face. What would he think? With a little cry, she pulled her head back and pushed at Stephen's chest, hard, with both hands, so that he almost toppled over backwards.

'No!' she cried. 'It's not going to work this time, Stephen. I don't care anything about you any more.'

He gave her the familiar crooked little-boy smile that used to melt her every resistance, and reached out for her again. 'You don't mean that, Nora.'

'Keep away, Stephen,' she said in a warning voice, backing off and holding up a hand.

He stopped short and stared, a hurt look on his face. 'I only want us to be together,' he said sulkily. 'I thought that's what you wanted, too. Hell, I've even left my wife for your sake.'

'I doubt that very much, Stephen,' she stated flatly. She narrowed her eyes at him. 'In fact, I'd be willing to bet she found out about another of your little escapades and kicked you out.'

From the deep flush that immediately began to spread over his pale features, Nora knew she had struck a chord. All she could think of now was how in the world she could ever have imagined she was in love with this shallow, self-seeking man.

'If you want my advice, you'll go back to your wife and try to patch things up with her. She's put up with you this long. She might even take you back if you begged her.'

'Who are you to give me advice?' he snarled.

Nora sighed. As usual he was turning ugly the minute he knew he wasn't going to get his own way. And she had used to find those childish moods attractive!

'I want you to leave now,' she said quietly.

He gave her one last long look. Apparently it had begun to sink in at last that she really meant it. He pulled his shoulders back in a feeble attempt at dignity, and walked past her towards the door. When he reached it he turned.

'This is your last chance, Nora,' he said in a lofty tone. 'I won't be back.'

'I'll risk it,' she retorted drily.

He opened the door, stepped outside, then banged it behind him. When she knew he was really gone, she ran over and slipped the chain bolt back on, then leaned back against the door, her eyes closed, breathing a deep sigh of relief.

Limp and exhausted from the emotional scene, she went over to the sideboard and, with hands that still shook, poured herself out what was left of her bottle of sherry. She stood there sipping it slowly until it began to work its magic on her nerves. The television was still on. She went over to switch it off, then sat down on the couch, lay her head back and closed her eyes.

As the tension gradually drained out of her, she thought again about Mark. Why, at just that critical moment, when she'd been teetering on the brink of giving in to Stephen, had his image flown into her mind?

It didn't matter. Whatever the reason, it had stopped her cold. Obviously she *did* care what he thought of her, cared a lot. As she mentally compared the two men, she opened her eyes and laughed aloud. They hardly belonged to the same species. It was like comparing solid gold with brass, or Michelangelo's 'David' with a 'Peanuts' cartoon.

Then her shoulders sagged. No use thinking along those lines. There was no future there. She'd made it abundantly clear to Mark how she felt about him. She thought about that one kiss he'd given her, the sweetness of it, no pressure, no demands.

She sighed. He wouldn't be satisfied with that for long, and she doubted she'd ever see him again in any case.

The following Friday morning Jackie burst into Nora's office, shut the door behind her, then whirled around, her hands on her hips.

'Well, if that doesn't take the cake!' she sputtered disgustedly. 'They've pulled some pretty shabby tricks in the past around here, but this beats all.'

Nora knew immediately what was wrong. 'I take it they've announced the name of the new director,' she said in a tight voice. Jackie only nodded. 'And it's not me.' Jackie nodded again.

It was a blow, but somehow Jackie's very vocal indignation seemed to create a kind of icy cold fatalism in Nora's mind. She put her elbows on top of her desk, cupped her chin in her hands and gave the redhead a rueful smile.

'Well, those are the breaks, I guess,' she said. 'If there's someone more qualified than I am——'

'Nuts to that!' Jackie exclaimed bitterly, sinking down in a chair. 'You're not going to believe this. A woman named Smith got the appointment. I never even heard of her, but apparently she has a handicap, if you want to call it that.'

Nora raised her shoulders resignedly. 'Well, Jackie, that's policy. You can't argue with the reasoning behind it. It's fair, after all, to give people a chance who——'

She stopped short when she saw Jackie raise a hand in the air to silence her. 'Wait!' she cried. 'You haven't heard what the handicap is.' She leapt to her feet, braced her hands on top of the desk and leaned over to fix Nora with a baleful look.

'Well?' Nora asked. 'Are you going to tell me what it is?'

'She's an alcoholic,' Jackie stated with grim satisfaction.

Nora's mouth fell open. 'An alcoholic?'

Jackie nodded. 'Can you believe it?' She shook her head slowly from side to side. 'Like you, I go along with the policy that gives an edge to disadvantaged people. But since when has alcoholism been a handicap? Well, I'm going to raise a ruckus about this that will rock the whole Internal Revenue Service.'

'Right. And get exactly nowhere,' Nora stated flatly. 'Listen, Jackie, you're going to do no such thing. The decision has been made, and there's nothing we can do about it.'

Jackie folded her arms in front of her and glared. 'You know the trouble with you, Nora, is that you're too damned passive. In this world you've got to fight for what you want. No one's going to hand you anything on a silver platter. Now, first we'll tackle Personnel, then——'

'No!' Nora said in a loud, firm voice. 'I'm not, and neither are you. It's not worth it. Please, Jackie, I mean it. The last thing I want to do is blow this into a big battle. It's done, and if I can live with it, so can you.'

Jackie stared at her for a long moment, then shook her head. 'OK,' she said at last. 'If that's the way you feel, Nora. You sound as though you really mean it. I don't agree with you, but if that's what you want...'

'It is.'

'Then I guess there's nothing more to say.'

Still shaking her head, she turned and strode out of the room. Nora sat there watching until she was gone. Then she got up from her desk and walked slowly over to the one small window. Now that she was alone, she could try to collect her own thoughts.

It had started to snow again, and as she stared out at the gently falling flakes she could almost physically feel her heart gradually sinking to the lowest ebb she could ever remember. She hadn't really realised just how much she was counting on that job until she'd found out she'd lost it. With her personal life a shambles and her relationships a mess, her career had come to seem like the one bright spot, the only reason even to get up in the morning.

Now that was gone, too. What was there for her? She was twenty-seven years old. She'd never reach a brilliant position in her work, never marry, never have children. At least Jackie had a husband and kids, while she didn't dare even allow herself to think about falling in love. The disasters that always led to didn't bear thinking about. She had nothing.

She stood there brooding over these dismal realities for a good quarter of an hour. The snowfall was thickening and a brisk wind had come up, slashing the icy flakes against the window-pane in a steady tattoo. The buses would be running late, taxis and cars would be stalled in the street, she'd drag home long after dark, tired, cold, wet and hungry.

Finally, she gave herself a little shake. She had piles of work on her desk. Maybe that would take her mind off her troubles, at least for the rest of the afternoon.

The trip home was every bit as gruelling as she had anticipated. First she had to stand at her stop in the swirling snow for an hour as one bus after another already crammed with desperate commuters anxious to get home passed her by. She was so numb emotionally by now that she hardly cared. There was nothing waiting for her at home except a cold, empty apartment.

When she finally did manage to squeeze herself on to a bus, it was so jam-packed with all the other people pressing against her that she could hardly breathe in the close air, which was musty and reeking of damp wool and wet leather. Inching along the snow-packed streets, at one point the bus skidded ominously to avoid a stalled car. A sharp, loud gasp went up among the other passengers, but Nora hardly reacted at all, except to catch her footing. What did she care if they crashed?

By the time they reached her stop it was almost eight o'clock, and the snow was still falling. She stepped off the bus and started to cross the street, still so wrapped in gloom that she didn't even see the oncoming car lose control and start sliding towards her until it was too late.

Suddenly, she felt something heavy hitting her from behind with such force that the next thing she knew she was lying flat on her back in the snow, her head literally bouncing on it. She couldn't breathe, and there was a throbbing pain shooting up her right leg, from her ankle to her hip.

Dimly she could hear voices, someone shouting, but she was so dazed from the impact that she could only lie there helplessly, her eyes squeezed shut tight, gasping and panting and struggling to get her breath. All she could think of was that she was going to die.

Then she heard someone calling her name, faintly, as though from a great distance. She opened her eyes and looked up. In the glow of the street-light, she made out a familiar face gazing down at her. She must be unconscious, she thought. It couldn't possibly be him. What in the world would Mark Leighton be doing in front of her apartment in a snowstorm?

and she tried to fight off unconsciousness, she thought, the accident must only be that, which in her mind would make it seem far too deep in dream of her past it was the snowstorm...

CHAPTER FOUR

'NORA,' she heard Mark say in a steady, reassuring voice. 'Can you tell me how badly you're hurt?'

Apparently it *was* Mark Leighton. Gingerly, she tested the muscles of her legs and arms. Except for the pain in her right leg, everything seemed to be in working order.

'I'm all right,' she said at last. 'I think.'

He nodded. 'The car just grazed you and knocked you down. If you're sure nothing is broken, we'd better get out of here before another one comes along.'

Sliding his arms under her knees and shoulders, he lifted her up gently, then carried her through the snow to the pavement and down the half-block to her building. When they reached the entrance, he stopped under the light and peered down at her, examining her carefully.

'How are you doing?' he asked quietly. 'I'm going to take you to a hospital. You may be more seriously injured than you realise.'

She shook her head. 'No, I'm fine. Really I am. My leg hurts a little, but I think mainly I had the wind knocked out of me. I just need a little time to get my bearings.'

Suddenly the shock of what had happened to her began to set in. She felt as though every ounce of energy were being drained out of her, leaking slowly away. An irresistible sensation of lassitude began to steal over her. As she gazed up at Mark's kind face, so full of concern, hot tears gathered and stung behind her eyes. 'Oh, Mark,' she wailed, as they spilled over and ran down her cheeks unchecked.

She raised her arms up around his neck, buried her face in his chest and sobbed like a child. It wasn't just the accident. That was only the last straw, the culmination of a whole series of events that were finally taking their toll.

'What is it?' Mark asked worriedly when she had cried herself out and begun to quiet down. 'Are you in pain? Is it your leg?'

She raised her tear-stained face to his and shook her head. 'No,' she choked out. 'It's my whole life.'

He smiled and bent his head to kiss her lightly on the forehead, then carried her into the building and up to her apartment. Once inside her living-room, he set her down carefully on the couch and helped her off with her jacket. He knelt down before her, and as he pulled off her right boot she winced with pain from the already swollen ankle, and couldn't quite suppress a little cry.

He gave her a stern look. 'I'm going to take you to a doctor now,' he stated flatly. He rose to his feet.

'No,' she said. 'Please. I don't need one.'

'Well, then, I can at least bind up that ankle. Do you have any adhesive tape?'

'Yes. In the bathroom, just down the hall.'

Even after he'd bound the ankle securely, it still throbbed, but she felt much better generally, safe and sound at least, and not too badly the worse for wear. Mark had gone into the kitchen to look for something to fix for their dinner, and she lay back now, her eyes closed, listening to him potter around in the next room.

'What I want to know,' she called to him, 'is what in the world you were doing at eight o'clock at night in the middle of a blizzard in front of my apartment.'

'It's a long story,' he called back.

He appeared in the doorway, tray in hand, and came over to set it down on the table beside the couch. Then he pulled up a chair across from her and sat down.

'You certainly have barren cupboards,' he said with a smile. 'I had a heck of a time finding anything edible in there.' He gestured towards the steaming bowls of soup, the plate of crackers. 'You can't live on canned soup, you know.'

'Oh, I don't have a great appetite,' she said.

'I can see that,' he commented, eyeing her critically. 'You look as though you've lost weight since the last time I saw you.'

She started to raise herself up to a sitting position, but he immediately leapt to his feet and came over to the couch before she could move a muscle.

'Here, let me help you,' he said.

He put his arm under her waist and carefully raised her up so that she could brace her back against the arm of the couch and still keep her legs stretched out. Then he set the tray on her lap and stood up, looking down at her.

'How's that?' he asked. 'Will you be able to manage all right?'

'Yes, thanks. I'm putting you to an awful lot of trouble. You'd better go eat your own while it's hot.'

She picked up her spoon and began to stir it around in the bowl of soup. Apparently satisfied that she really was going to eat, he went back to his chair, sat down and started eating.

'You haven't answered my question,' she said, still stirring.

'What question?' he asked between spoonfuls.

'How you happened to be here in the first place.'

He finished up the last spoonful of soup and leaned back in his chair. 'Well,' he said slowly, 'it's quite simple. The truth is I just wanted to see you.'

'But you haven't even called me in over a month.'

He shrugged. 'Well, after what happened the last time, I was afraid that if I called too soon you might refuse to see me, so I decided to come in person and try to catch you when you came home from work.' He grinned broadly. 'I just picked a bad day for it. Or a good one, depending on how you look at it.'

She smiled. 'Well, good for me, at any rate.'

'At least I got in.' He pointed at her untasted bowl of soup. 'Come on, now. Eat that before it gets cold.'

When she finally did start to eat, it tasted so good that she cleaned it up in short order. In the meantime, Mark had risen to his feet and gone over to the chair by the front door where he had hung his heavy jacket. Nora turned to watch him as he started to shrug into it.

'Where are you going?' she asked in alarm. 'You're not leaving me!'

'Of course not,' he replied. 'I'm just going out to get something more substantial to eat. I noticed an all-night grocery store around the corner while I was waiting for you to come home earlier. I won't be long.'

'Please don't,' she said. 'Not yet. The soup was enough for now. Maybe later. I—I don't want you to leave me alone.'

Slowly, he removed his arm from the sleeve and laid the jacket back down on the chair. Then he crossed over to the couch and stood there looking down at her for several long seconds, frowning.

'Listen,' he said at last. 'I'm going to have to insist you see a doctor. You might be hurt more badly than you realise.'

'No,' she said quickly, then added, 'Maybe tomorrow, if it's not any better.'

'Do you have anything to drink? Brandy? Whisky?'

'What I'd really like is a cup of coffee. There's a jar of instant in the cupboard where you found the soup.'

He nodded and went into the kitchen. While he was gone, Nora lay her head back on the pillow again and closed her eyes, wondering how she could talk him into spending the night with her. The thought of being alone was more than she could bear. The couch she was lying on could be made into a comfortable bed. She'd sleep in it herself and give him her room if he'd agree to stay.

When she heard him come back, she sat up again and watched him. He looked wonderful to her, a lifesaver, and she was grateful beyond words for his quiet, reassuring presence. He was carrying two steaming mugs of coffee, and after he handed one to her he sat back down in his chair and took a sip.

'Mark,' she said after she'd drunk about half a cup. 'I want to thank you again for all you've done, just for being there to help me tonight.' He waved a hand dismissively in the air, but before he could say anything, she rushed on. 'I wonder if I could impose on you even more.'

'Sure. Just name it.'

She bit her lip and frowned down at her hands for a moment, then raised her head to face him again. 'Would you consider staying here tonight?' she blurted out. 'You can sleep in my bed. I don't mind the couch and——'

She stopped short because he had burst into loud laughter. 'Listen,' he said between gusts. 'Do you think for one moment I'd leave you alone tonight? I was just trying to think of a way of suggesting I stay without offending you. And you'll sleep in your own bed. I don't mind the couch.'

She heaved a deep sigh of sheer relief. 'Well, that's all right then,' she said. 'I can never thank you enough...'

'No. Don't thank me. It's my pleasure.' He set his empty mug down on the tray and leaned forward in his chair, his elbows braced on his knees, his hands clasped between them. 'Now,' he said. 'Tell me about your life.'

She gazed blankly at him. 'What?'

'You said your whole life hurt. Why?'

She flushed with embarrassment as she recalled the tearful scene out on the street after the accident, the shameful admission of weakness. 'I was in shock,' she muttered.

'No, you weren't. Come on. You'll feel better if you talk about it. I make a good father confessor. Try me.'

'Well, it's not really as bad as I made it sound. I've already told you about my bad luck with men, and I thought I'd come to terms with it, that things were going rather well for me. Then today I found out the job I'd been hoping to get, was even counting on, went to someone else.'

Then she told him about being passed over for the appointment as director, the woman with the alcoholic 'handicap' who'd been given the job, and when she was through his face was creased with a stern, indignant frown.

'I'm going to take some steps to remedy that situation,' he said in a flat, positive tone. 'I have a little clout with the congressman from our district, and he owes me a favour or two.'

'No, Mark,' she said firmly. 'There's nothing anyone can do. Besides, it's not only the job. That was just the last straw. It seems as though everything that could go wrong in my life has managed to do so in the past few months. It's as though there's a little grey cloud following me around wherever I go. I can't seem to get out from under.'

She was trying to smile, to make a joke of it, but by the time she'd finished her little speech she could hear her voice start to quiver. Quickly she turned her head away as the waves of self-pity came crashing over her, hating herself for her weakness, but helplessly unable to ward it off.

He didn't say anything for several long moments. Then she heard him clear his throat, the creak of his chair. By then she had herself under control and she turned to face him. He had risen to his feet and was standing by the couch looking down at her, his hands in the pockets of his dark trousers, a troubled look on his face.

'Sorry,' she said with a weak smile. 'I'm not normally such a baby.'

He waved a hand in the air. 'Listen, you're still suffering from shock. What you need most of all now is rest. It's time you got to bed.'

She started to lift her legs up off the couch, but before she could swing them over the side Mark had leaned down to pick her up, and the next thing she knew she was in his arms being carried out into the short hallway that led to the one bedroom and bathroom.

The door to her bedroom was open. Once inside he set her down carefully on top of the bed, then reached over to switch on the lamp beside it. He stood there for a while staring down at the table. Nora glanced over. Stephen's picture was still there. She'd forgotten all about it.

Without comment, he turned to her. 'Do you have any aspirin?'

She raised her head. 'Yes, there should be some in the bathroom cabinet across the hall.'

He nodded. 'I'll just be a minute.'

When he was gone, she propped herself up on her pillows and leaned back with a sigh. As she listened to him pottering in the bathroom, it suddenly struck her how odd it was to have this strange man going through her most personal belongings.

But he didn't *seem* strange. He had been there when she'd needed him, taken charge so effortlessly and naturally that she couldn't think of another person in the world she could possibly have felt safer with.

There was something about his quiet strength, so utterly at her disposal, that reassured her, made her feel safe, protected, even pampered. Somehow she was convinced that she could trust him no matter what. She'd never felt that way about any of the men she knew. It was an entirely new experience for her, and, although it was very pleasant to be taken care of this way, she had no idea what it all meant or how to take it.

He was only gone a few minutes, and when he came back he was carrying a bottle of aspirin in one hand and a glass of water in the other. He set the glass down on the table beside the bed, opened the bottle and looked at her.

'How many?' he asked.

'One should do it,' she replied. 'I don't take them very often.'

'Try two.'

He shook them out and handed them to her, then gave her the water glass and watched her while she swallowed them down.

'I'll leave them here,' he said when she gave him back the glass. 'In case you need more during the night.'

'Thanks, Mark.'

'Now, do you think you can manage all right on your own?' he asked. 'I mean, to get undressed and into bed.'

'Oh, yes,' she replied hurriedly. 'As you can see, it's quite a small room. Everything's almost within arm's reach.' She gave him a wicked smile. 'But thanks for the offer.'

He returned the smile and raised his broad shoulders in a diffident shrug. 'I told you I live with my mother and sister. I'm used to women in a state of undress. If it wouldn't bother you, it certainly won't bother me.'

'No, thanks. I think I can manage by hanging on to things.'

'Don't you have something you can use for a cane?'

She thought a minute. 'Well, there's a pretty sturdy umbrella in my closet. If you'd get that for me I can try using it out.' He crossed over to the wardrobe, found the umbrella and came back and handed it to her.

'Do you want me to stick around while you practise?' he asked.

She shook her head. 'You'll hear me if I fall.'

'I'll say goodnight, then. Yell if you need anything during the night. Otherwise I'll see you in the morning.'

'Goodnight, Mark. And thanks again for everything.' He turned to go, and when he reached the door she called to him, 'You'll find sheets and blankets in the hall closet if you want to make up a bed.'

When he was gone, she slid her hips slowly off the bed, putting all her weight on her good leg and balancing herself with the support of the umbrella. Gingerly she tried putting some weight on her right foot. It was painful, but, after a few tries, she found she was able to hobble around the room if she took it slowly.

She limped across the hall to the bathroom, and on the way she could hear the television playing softly in the living-room. It sounded like a ball game of some kind, and once again she was struck by the incongruity of having this man here, spending the night, making himself so much at home.

After she'd washed the best she could, she went back to the bedroom, got undressed and put on her nightgown. Then she slipped under the covers and switched out the lamp by the side of the bed. She lay there staring up blankly at the dark ceiling and thinking over the events of the exhausting, traumatic evening.

In a matter of seconds, her eyes began to close. Her last thought before she drifted into a heavy, dreamless sleep was of Mark Leighton, just down the hall in her living-room, and how safe she felt just knowing he was there.

The next morning Nora awakened to the delicious mingled aroma of bacon frying and coffee perking. For a moment she couldn't think where it was coming from or who was cooking it. When she shifted her position, however, twisting her right ankle slightly, the throbbing pain in it jogged her memory. Mark Leighton had spent the night on the couch in her living-room.

She sat up abruptly, suddenly appalled at what she had done. Last night, when she'd been stunned, frightened, hurt, his presence had seemed like a godsend. Now, however, in the bright light of day, she felt a swift onset of anxiety. The man was a stranger. How on earth was she going to face him?

She eased herself out of bed and, when she cautiously tested her injured ankle, it didn't seem to be quite so painful as it had last night. With the help of her umbrella-cane, she managed to get dressed and washed, her teeth brushed and hair combed in only about twice the usual time it took her.

She hobbled down the hall towards the kitchen, stopping at the doorway. When she saw him standing at the counter, dressed in his dark trousers, tieless, his white shirt open at the throat and the sleeves rolled up to his elbows, her nerve almost failed her. It had been a long time, months, since a man had been inside her apartment, and Mark was so *large*. Much bigger than Stephen or any of the other men in her life. Somehow, seeing him standing there wielding a long fork and poking at the bacon sizzling before him on the stove, made her feel very small and vulnerable.

Through the kitchen window she could see that the sun was brightly shining, glaring down on the snow-covered roof across the way, the sky a brilliant cerulean blue.

Suddenly he turned around. When he saw her, his eyes lit up and he smiled, a brilliant flash of white teeth against his dark skin. He seemed so glad to see her, and that smile, so warm and welcoming, relieved her anxiety in a moment.

He was wiping his hands on a towel and crossing the room towards her. 'Good morning, merry sunshine,' he said.

'Good morning,' she said. 'How did you sleep?'

'Oh, I can sleep anywhere,' he said. 'How's the leg feeling this morning?'

'Better, I think.'

'Well, breakfast is almost ready. I went out shopping while you were asleep. Sit down and I'll dish it up. Then we're going to get you to a doctor.'

'I really don't think I need to see a doctor,' she said, limping towards the table on her umbrella.

He eyed her with an amused quirk of his eyebrows. 'Oh, no? We can talk about that after we've eaten.'

She eased herself on to one of the chairs at the table. 'I don't usually eat much breakfast,' she said.

'I know,' he rejoined curtly. He eyed her up and down. 'That's obvious. But you can try.'

Obediently, she tucked in. To her own amazement she wolfed down a glass of orange juice, two eggs, three rashers of bacon and two pieces of toast. When she was through she pushed her plate away and leaned back in her chair, sighing with contentment.

'That was wonderful, Mark. I wonder why food tastes so much better when someone else cooks it.'

He was gazing at her thoughtfully. 'You know what you need?'

'Well,' she said with a laugh, 'I can think of lots of things, but what do you have in mind?'

He braced his elbows on the table and leaned towards her. 'You need someone to take care of you.'

The look in his dark eyes was so serious, the expression on his face so sober, that her heart caught in her throat. Suddenly, he rose to his feet and came to stand over her. He braced his hands on the arms of her chair and leaned over her, looking into her eyes.

'I could take care of you, Nora,' he said huskily.

As his head came down, she closed her eyes. She knew he was going to kiss her, and when she felt his mouth on hers, warm, mobile, his lips opening and closing gently over hers, a pleasant glow filled her whole being. As the kiss deepened, became more demanding, with more of desire in it than tenderness, he put a hand at the base of her throat, letting it rest there, just above the swell of her breast.

He raised his head and looked down at her, his eyes searching hers. 'Nora?' he said softly.

She smiled. 'That was nice, Mark.'

'Shall I do it again?'

'Well, maybe not right now,' she said with a laugh.

He opened his mouth, as though to speak, but apparently thought better of it. Instead, he dropped his eyes from hers, cleared his throat, then carried his dish over to the sink and ran water into it.

'Do you have a doctor you see regularly?' he called over his shoulder.

She watched him in genuine amusement. He had obviously been taken completely off guard that she had allowed the kiss. More, that she had enjoyed it. At that moment, she felt it would be the easiest thing in the world to fall in love with this man. No one in her life had ever treated her with such tender affection and consideration. He was a dying breed.

'Yes,' she replied at last. 'Dr Banks. He's been our family doctor ever since I was born. Brought me into the world, treated me for measles and chicken-pox, and generally looked after the whole family.' She picked up her own dishes and started to struggle to her feet so she could carry them to the sink.

'Here, I'll do that,' he said, coming towards her. 'You sit down and rest that ankle.' He took the dishes from her and went back to the sink. 'Why don't you call him and see if he can take a look at that ankle this morning while I clear up in here?'

'Oh, I don't think I need——'

He turned around. 'Please,' he said. 'Humour me.'

She hesitated. 'All right,' she said. 'I guess it can't hurt anything.' She laughed. 'You've been such a good Samaritan that I guess I owe you that, if it'll make you feel better.'

After she'd called Dr Banks and he'd agreed to see her as soon as she could get to his office, Mark went out to put the chains on his car and warm it up while Nora got ready to go.

By the time he came back inside, stamping the snow off his feet, his nose and ears brick-red from the cold, her ankle was throbbing again from all the pressure she'd put on it that morning, and when Mark picked her up to carry her out to the car she didn't even think to object.

Outside, the air was fresh and cold, and everything in sight was covered with a heavy white blanket. There wasn't a trace of a cloud in the sky, and the pale winter sun glared down out of a bright blue sky, glittering off the crystalline snow packed on the ground and rooftops.

Since it was Saturday morning, the streets of the city were fairly clear of traffic, with only a few brave souls out on necessary errands. The doctor's surgery was only half a mile or so away from Nora's apartment, and although Mark drove cautiously it took less than fifteen minutes to get there.

Dr Banks could see her right away, and, while Nora followed him into the examining-room, Mark settled himself on a chair in the waiting-room with the morning paper.

'Well, you gave that a nice twist,' the doctor said after he'd finished examining her ankle. 'You say you were hit by a car?'

She nodded. 'Yes. Last night on my way home from work as I was crossing the street from the bus-stop. I didn't even see it coming. It just slid out of control in the snow, and I happened to be in its way.'

'Well, it's not serious. No bones broken. Just a slight sprain. Better stay off your feet as much as possible for a few weeks, and you'll be as good as new. I'll lend you a cane you can use. No need for crutches, they'd only get in your way. You can use the leg, but keep as much pressure off it as possible.'

'Well, that's a relief,' she said. 'I'm glad it's nothing more complicated than that.'

She was about to rise to her feet to go, but he was looking at her with an odd expression of disapproval on his round, lined face. 'When was the last time you were in for a check-up?' he asked abruptly.

'Oh, I don't know. It must be a few years.'

He raised his bushy white eyebrows. 'A few years? More like five or six, I'd say.' Although the blue eyes behind his gold-rimmed glasses were kindly, there was a stern note to his voice. 'You're far too thin, Nora, and I don't like your colour.'

'Well, I don't have a great appetite,' she said defensively.

He rose to his feet. 'As soon as that ankle heals, I want you to make an appointment for a thorough physical.'

'All right.' She nodded meekly and got awkwardly to her feet.

He went to a cupboard, took out a sturdy wooden cane and came back to hand it to her. 'Here,' he said. 'This should help.'

She limped before him back out into the waiting-room. When the door opened, Mark rose to his feet and came walking towards her. Nora introduced the two men, and, after a few pleasantries about the weather, the doctor vanished back into his office.

'Well?' Mark said as they walked slowly towards the outer door. 'What's the verdict?'

'You were right. It's only a mild sprain. He gave me this cane to use and told me to stay off my feet as much as possible for a few weeks.' She laughed drily. 'He also agreed with you that I was too thin, and is insisting I come in for a physical when the ankle is better.'

'Sounds like good advice,' he said, opening the door for her. 'Especially since he agrees with me,' he added with a grin.

Outside, Mark automatically turned to her, all ready to pick her up and carry her to the car, but she insisted on trying out the cane herself. After a short, rather heated discussion he finally gave in, but stayed close by her side over the slushy pavement, opened the car door for her and they got inside.

'See?' she said as he started the engine. 'I did make it on my own. This cane beats that umbrella. In fact, it makes me feel rather dignified.'

He didn't reply to that, nor did he speak again all the way home. He was scowling in concentration, apparently deep in thought, as he manoeuvred through the slick streets. The traffic had picked up slightly by now, and Nora assumed he was so silent because he had to focus all his attention on his driving.

When they arrived back at her apartment, once again she insisted on getting from the car to the building without his help, over his strenuous objections.

'You're a stubborn little thing,' he said when they reached her door. 'How can I convince you that it's far less trouble for me to carry you than it would be if you were to fall again?'

'Listen,' she said, when they were inside her apartment and shedding their outdoor clothing, 'if I have to stay off my feet for two weeks, I'd darned well better get used to getting around on my own. You won't be around after today, remember?'

He didn't respond to that. 'How about some coffee?' he asked, heading for the kitchen.

'Sounds good,' she replied as she followed him. 'But why don't you let me make it? I have one more favour to ask you before you go.' She grinned at him. 'I want to take full advantage of you while you're still here.'

'What is it?' he asked tersely.

'If I make out a shopping-list, would you mind going out to pick up some groceries for me? I don't think I can quite manage that on my own just yet.'

He stood a few feet away from her, his chin in his hand, gazing out the window with a faraway look in his eyes. Then, as though suddenly making up his mind to something, he turned to her, a set, determined expression on his face.

'Let's sit down for a minute,' he said, gesturing towards the table. 'I want to talk to you about something.'

'That sounds ominous,' she said with a smile. 'But OK.'

When they were seated, he leaned back in his chair and fixed her with a direct look. 'I really should get back home today,' he announced in a curt tone.

'I know,' she replied quickly. 'I can probably have the groceries delivered. You've already done so much——'

'I want you to come with me,' he broke in abruptly.

CHAPTER FIVE

NORA stared at Mark, her mouth half open, her eyes wide. Was he serious? Apparently so. His square chin jutted out determinedly and his gaze was steady.

'I can't do that, Mark,' she said softly.

'Why not?'

She shrugged. 'Well——' She laughed nervously. 'I don't know. I just can't.'

He leaned towards her, his elbows propped on the table-top. 'I think there's more wrong with you than a sprained ankle, and apparently your doctor agrees with me. You said yourself he told you you were too thin. You're not going to be able to go to work anyway. A few weeks at the farm will be good for you. Just get away from the city altogether.' His hard features softened into a smile. 'My sister loves to wait on invalids.'

'Mark, I'm not an invalid.'

He waved a hand in the air. 'Well, whatever. The point is she won't object, if that's what's worrying you. In fact, she'd be delighted. And I want you to come.'

That look was back in his eyes, and Nora immediately grew wary. A few friendly, really quite brotherly kisses were one thing, going to stay at his house quite another. Was he expecting some kind of payment for his Good Samaritan act?

'Mark,' she said slowly. 'I've made it as clear to you as I possibly could that I'm definitely, positively not in the market for any kind of—well—serious relationship.' She reddened. 'You know what I mean.'

He spread his hands. 'Who's talking about that? We're friends, aren't we?' She nodded. 'And I came to your rescue last night, didn't I?' She nodded again. 'Then why not do me this favour? No strings, no commitment, no involvement. Please, Nora.'

Nora searched his face. The hungry look was gone, and in its place was an expression so earnest, so sincere, so guileless that she had to believe him. She lowered her eyes to stare down at her hands, trying to think. What was the right thing to do, for her and Mark?

As she pondered the implications of this sudden, totally unexpected invitation, she had to admit that the prospect of two weeks away was very tempting. Away from the city, her apartment, the office, the job she didn't get. And away from Stephen.

He pushed his chair back and gave her a hopeful, expectant look. 'I'll call Anna now and tell her you're coming. OK?'

She raised her eyes to meet his. 'OK,' she said at last. 'But only if you're sure you understand——'

He raised a hand to stop her, grinning broadly now. 'I promise. Don't even mention the subject again,' he said firmly. He started out of the room towards the telephone in the hall. When he reached the door, he turned around. 'Besides,' he said lightly, 'if I break my promise, all you have to do is say no.'

Before she could think up a reply to that enigmatic statement, he was gone, and the next thing she heard was his low, muffled voice on the telephone in the hall.

She got up and hobbled over to the stove, ran water into the kettle and put it on the burner for the coffee. While it heated, she sat down again and thought over all the things she'd have to do to get ready to go.

Her apartment would be all right. The few houseplants she'd been given in the past had all long since expired, she had no animals, and the building was secure enough. She'd have to pack. What? Country clothes. Trousers, warm sweaters, comfortable shoes. What about her job? She could call Jackie and ask her to fix things up for her on Monday at the office.

Mark came back just then, beaming. 'Anna is delighted I'm bringing you back with me,' he announced. He sat down next to her. 'In fact, if I know my sister, by now she's in the downstairs guest room making up the bed for you.'

'I've been thinking, Mark,' she began in a worried voice.

He held up a hand. 'It's too late to change your mind. Anna would never speak to me again.'

She laughed nervously. 'No, it's not that. I was just thinking of all the things I have to do, you know, packing——'

Just then the shrill ringing of the telephone cut her off in mid-sentence, and Mark jumped to his feet. 'I'll get that for you.'

'Better not,' she said, gripping the arms of her chair to lever herself upright. 'I can think of several people who would never give me another moment's peace if they called here on Saturday morning and a man answered the phone.' She smiled. 'You can make the coffee.'

She took hold of her cane, limped out into the hall, picked up the receiver and said hello.

'Hello, Nora?' came a faint voice. 'This is your mother.'

'Mother, where in the world are you?'

'We're in Paris, darling. I just wanted to call to tell you we'll be heading home in a few days. Your father has had all the travelling he can stand.'

'Well, I'll be glad to see you, of course,' Nora said. 'Will you be coming back to Washington?'

'Yes. We're thinking about looking for a condominium, someplace where we don't have anything to tie us down. Now, how have you been, darling?'

'Oh, all right. Well, actually,' she went on with a little laugh, 'I did have a slight accident. Nothing serious, just a spill in the snow and a slight sprain.'

'Darling, I'm so sorry. Can you get around all right? How about your job?'

'I have lots of leave coming, and some friends of mine have invited me to spend a few weeks with them at their farm in Virginia. In fact we were just leaving. Hang on a second, and I'll get you their number in case you need to call me.'

She put her hand firmly over the receiver to muffle her voice and called to Mark. He appeared in the doorway, his eyebrows raised in a question. She asked him for his telephone number, and when he told her she repeated it into the telephone.

'All right. I've got that,' her mother said. 'Now tell me about these friends of yours. Do I know them? What kind of farm do they have?'

Nora sighed. Leave it to her inquisitive mother to start probing for social status immediately. 'Their name is Leighton and their farm is in the western part of Virginia. They raise thoroughbred horses and grow apples.'

'That sounds prosperous.' She paused. 'I think I've heard the name.'

'Will you be coming directly to Washington, Mother?' Nora put in hurriedly.

'No. We plan to spend a week or so with friends in New York first. I'll call you from there. How long will you be away?'

'I'm not sure. Why don't you try here first?'

'All right. Well, I'd better hang up now. These transatlantic calls cost a fortune, and your father is giving me dirty looks.'

'Goodbye, then, Mother. Thanks for calling. And give my love to Daddy.'

After she hung up she dialled Jackie's home number. Mark had tactfully gone back to the kitchen, so she was able to tell Jackie her plans in the same guarded terms as she had her mother.

It only took her half an hour to pack, and they were ready to leave by eleven o'clock.

Mark's farm was a good two-hour drive from Washington, through the small towns and rolling hills of Virginia to the westernmost part of the state. The further away they came from the city, the less snow they saw, but it was still a bleak, wintry landscape until, after the first two hours or so, a tree-

covered mountain range began to loom up in the
distance.

'Those are the Blue Ridge Mountains straight
ahead,' Mark pointed out as he drove.

'Well, they do look blue, don't they?' Nora commented. 'Especially in the sunshine. How far is it
to your place?'

'Just over the mountains, down in the
Shenandoah Valley.' He darted her a quick sideways
look. 'Why? Are you getting tired?'

She met his glance and smiled. 'No. Just a little
nervous. Won't your family think it odd to have a
perfect stranger barging in on them this way? And
a crippled one, at that.'

'I told you. Anna was delighted I was bringing
you. Don't worry about it—there are people coming
and going at our place all the time. It's like that in
the country.'

She had to take his word for it, but with each
passing mile she grew edgier. It wasn't only her fear
of intruding on Mark's family. The further away
she was from home, the more she doubted the
wisdom of her impulsive decision to accept Mark's
invitation.

She hardly knew the man. Well, that wasn't quite
true. She knew enough about him to be certain he
meant her no harm. But she had put herself pretty
much at his mercy. Hardly able to hobble around
even with the help of a cane, how would she be able
to get home except with his help?

She knew nothing about farm life or com-
munities. For all she knew he could be taking her
to a tumbledown shack where everyone slept in the

same room and pigs and chickens wandered in and out at will. Or a log cabin. A trailer!

She didn't realise how tensed up she'd become from these horrific images until she felt Mark's hand cover hers and she glanced down to see that she was gripping the edge of her seat so tightly that her knuckles were white.

'Relax, will you?' he said softly. He gave her hand a warm squeeze, then removed it. 'My family will love you. Why shouldn't they? You're a warm, friendly, likeable person. And you look great. I like that red dress. The colour suits you.'

She'd had a hard time deciding what to wear. Going to the country seemed to require rough, outdoor clothes—jeans, sweaters, woollen shirts— but since Mark still had on his dark business suit, she'd put on the red dress to fit in with it.

After a few more miles he turned to her again. 'Are you hungry?'

'Not very. Not after that enormous breakfast you cooked.'

He glanced at his watch. 'It's just past noon, and we only have less than an hour to go. Think you can wait?'

'Sure.'

They were winding upwards now, on the wide, scenic road that curved along the crest of the mountain range. Somehow the snowstorm that had hit Washington the previous day had missed this part of the state, and, although there were still patches of old greyish snow here and there in the higher elevations, the road was clear.

Once down in the valley on the other side of the summit, the terrain levelled out and cultivated farmlands began to appear. Even in the dead of winter, the neat white houses and farm buildings, the grassy pastures and tall grain silos were picturesque and inviting. The orchards were only rows of bare brown stumps now, but she could well imagine how beautiful they would be in the spring when the trees began to leaf out.

Soon, Mark turned off the main highway on to a narrow side road and drove about half a mile until he came to a wide metal gate, painted white and set in a tall fence that seemed to stretch for miles on either side. At the top of the gate, curving capital letters spelled out the name 'LEIGHTONS'.

Mark stopped the car, reached into the glove compartment, took out a small metal box and pressed a button. The gate swung slowly open, to reveal a long, curving paved drive straight ahead. He drove through, pressed the button again, and the gate closed behind them.

Nora was so struck by the beauty of the scene rising up before her eyes as they drove that it literally took her breath away. She sat bolt upright in her seat and gaped open-mouthed at the wide expanse of green lawn, the clumps of evergreen shrubs, the tall trees, the neat white buildings.

Just ahead was the house itself, a sprawling two-storey structure, also painted white, with dark green shutters at the windows. A wide, covered veranda stretched across the front, and as she watched she saw a woman appear there. She had just come out of the front door and was wiping her hands on a towel. Then she raised one hand to shield her eyes from the bright sunshine and started waving at them with the other.

A tumbledown shack! A log cabin! A trailer! She couldn't possibly have been more off base! She turned to Mark. He was gazing at her, an amused smile curling on his lips.

'Is it what you expected?' he asked as he pulled up in front of the house.

'Not exactly,' she said.

As soon as he switched off the engine and got out of the car, the woman on the veranda ran towards him, and Nora watched through the front windscreen as she flung herself into his arms. Mark kissed her fondly on the cheek and, with one arm still around her, led her over to Nora's side of the car.

As they approached, Nora was struck by the similarity between them. Their colouring was exactly the same: black hair, rather dark complexion, and she was also tall, at least as tall as Nora herself, but with a much sturdier, heavier bone-structure. She wore her long hair pulled back in a rather untidy bun at the back of her neck, and was wearing a pair of dark woollen trousers and a heavy red sweater.

When they reached the car she stepped aside, while Mark opened Nora's door and reached in to take her by the arm and help her get out. Once outside, she stood there, feeling rather shy, leaning on her cane, while Mark introduced the two women.

'Nora, this is my sister, Anna. Anna, Nora Chambers.'

'I'm so pleased you could come,' Anna said with a broad, welcoming smile. She grasped Nora's free hand and clasped it warmly in both of hers.

'Thank you,' Nora replied. 'It seems like a terrible imposition, but Mark——'

'Nonsense!' Anna cried. 'I was delighted when he called. We don't get much company in the winter except for local people, and I'm always glad to meet any friend of Mark's.' She glanced down at Nora's ankle. 'Mark said you'd had an accident. How is the leg?'

'Well, aside from the fact that it'll be useless for a while, it's not so bad. Your brother was a lifesaver. He seemed to know just what to do with it.'

'Oh, he's used to dealing with leg injuries,' Anna said with a wave of her hand. 'The horses, you know.' She clapped a hand over her mouth. 'I'm sorry. I didn't mean that the way it sounded.'

By now Mark was roaring with laughter. He put an arm around his sister's shoulders. 'You do have a way with words, Anna,' he said, still choking.

Nora was laughing herself by now, and, the ice effectively broken, the three of them started walking slowly towards the house. By the time they reached it, a man and woman Nora assumed were Mark's parents had appeared at the doorway.

They were a study in contrasts. The man was so much like Mark—tall, dark, heavily muscled, with broad, prominent features—that there was no mistaking the relationship. But the woman was the exact opposite—small, slim, with fading light blonde hair and a pale complexion. As they came closer, Nora could see that her eyes were a faded greyish-blue.

'Mother, Dad, this is Nora Chambers,' Mark said.

They welcomed her just as warmly as his sister had, and, although she still felt somewhat strange, by now Nora was convinced that it would be all right, that they really did want her here.

They all went inside into a wide, tiled entry hall. There was a heavy oak table along one wall, a large framed mirror above it, and a coat rack in one corner. Leading off it to the right was a huge living-room, with a brick fireplace at the far end where a log fire was blazing merrily. On the left, a wide, gracefully curving oak staircase led up to the second floor.

As Mark carried in her suitcase and they shed their heavy clothing, everyone seemed to be talking at once, asking Nora about her accident, filling Mark in on various crises that had arisen during his absence. Nora gazed from one to the other. Raised as an only child and living alone for so many years, she found the presence of all these people rather overwhelming.

'Let's go in the living-room,' Anna said, taking her by the arm to lead the way. 'We can have our lunch in front of the fire. You two must be starved.'

'We waited lunch for you,' her mother said. 'Or did you stop somewhere along the way?'

Mark and his father, already deep in a conversation about horses, had gone on ahead. Nora looked after his tall, retreating figure in dismay. It seemed as though her one source of support had suddenly vanished, and she wondered what in the world she was doing here in the midst of all these strangers.

'As a matter of fact,' she said hesitantly, hanging back, 'I'm really more tired than I am hungry.'

'Oh, of course!' Anna cried. 'How thoughtless of me! You must still be feeling the effects of your accident. I'd forgotten it only happened last night.'

Her mother was shaking her head sympathetically. 'And it's such a long trip from Washington. You must be exhausted.'

'Mark!' Anna called to her brother.

He turned around and came walking back into the hall. 'Yes?'

'I think Nora wants to rest a while. I've put her in the downstairs guest room so she won't have to climb all those steps. Why don't you take her there and I'll fix her lunch on a tray?'

He nodded. 'Good idea.' He turned to Nora and gave her a warm, slow smile. 'Shall I carry you?'

'No,' she replied hurriedly. 'No, I can manage.' She turned to Anna. 'I'm sorry to be so much trouble. It's just that——'

'Don't you dare apologise!' Anna cried. 'You came here to rest, and that's what you're going to do.' She looked at her brother. 'Go on, Mark.'

Mark picked up her suitcase and led Nora through a doorway behind the staircase the opposite side of the hall and down a long corridor until they came to a half-open door. Mark pushed it open to reveal a large, pleasant bedroom, papered in a flowery pattern and with more heavy oak furniture. By the window sat a small round table with two comfortable chairs drawn up to it.

'What a lovely room!' Nora exclaimed when they were inside.

Mark set her suitcase down on a chair, crossed over to a door and opened it. 'There's a bathroom in here,' he said. 'You'll have all the privacy you

need.' He came back to stand before her. 'I'm sorry
if the family was too much for you to swallow all
at once. They do tend to come on a little strong,
but they mean well.'

'Not at all,' she assured him. 'They're very kind.'

He laughed. 'Ah, but you haven't even seen the
worst. Wait until you meet Tony.'

She had started unpacking her suitcase, but
turned to him now with an enquiring look. 'Tony?'

'Yes, my younger brother. He handles all the
business end of the farm and is gone most of the
time. I'm hoping he'll get back in time to meet you,
but with Tony you never know.'

'Are you and he alike?'

'We're about as different as brothers could possibly be. He's the brains of the family, the sharp
one, the world traveller, the smooth-talker. I'm the
dull one who stays at home and does all the manual
labour.' He moved towards the door. 'Now, I'll give
you some time to get settled while I get our lunch.'

By now she was swaying on her feet. 'I'm really
more tired than I am hungry at the moment,' she
said apologetically.

'Of course,' he said. He went over to the bed and
pulled down the quilt. 'Why don't you lie down
now and try to get some sleep? Do you need any
aspirin? I'm sure there's some in the bathroom.'

'No. I'll be fine.'

'Well, then, I'll check back in an hour or so to
see if you want something to eat.'

'Thanks, Mark.'

He hesitated for a moment, as though he wanted
to say more, but with a brief nod he turned and
went out of the door, closing it quietly behind him.

When he was gone, she quickly shrugged out of the red dress and hung it in the wardrobe, slipped off her shoes and stockings and limped into the bathroom barefoot to wash.

Then she climbed wearily up on top of the bed and pulled the quilt over her. Within seconds she was sound asleep.

When she woke up again, it was just beginning to get dark outside. For a moment she couldn't think where she was. She raised her head and looked around. Through the window a pale, dusky glow cast just enough light into the shadowy room to orientate her.

She was at Mark's farm. She yawned and stretched, then nestled back on the pillow with a sigh of contentment and closed her eyes again. With only her slip on, the room was a little chilly, and she pulled the heavy quilt up over her bare shoulders.

After a moment there came a knock on the door. 'Nora!' she heard Mark calling to her in a low voice. 'Are you awake?'

'Yes, Mark,' she replied. 'Come on in.'

She sat up in bed, propping a pillow behind her. The door opened and he came inside. He walked over to the bed and stood there looking down at her.

'Had a good nap?'

'Oh, yes. I zonked out the minute my head hit the pillow.'

It suddenly dawned on her what she must look like—her hair messy, without a trace of make-up and only half dressed. She ran a hand through her hair to straighten out the tangles and tightened the quilt around her shoulders.

She laughed apologetically. 'I must look a mess.'

'You look beautiful,' he said.

The laughter died on her lips when she saw the look in his eyes. Slowly he lowered himself down on the bed. Then he leaned towards her and kissed her lightly on the mouth, a friendly, unthreatening kiss. His soft, warm mouth tasted of toothpaste, and he'd obviously shaved and bathed while she'd been asleep. He smelled like fresh soap, and his cheek was barely rough against hers.

She closed her eyes as he shifted his weight on the bed to move closer to her. There was no urgency in his kiss, and no fireworks went off in her head. There was only a steady, reassuring warmth that lulled her completely and made her feel lazily content, like a sleek, purring cat.

His mouth left hers and he ran a hand over her hair. 'You are beautiful, you know,' he said huskily.

She smiled at him. 'No, I'm not. But I'm glad you think so.'

The deep brown eyes lit up. 'Are you?'

She nodded. His arms came around her then, pulling her up against him, and as the quilt slipped away she felt his hands, warm and strong, on her bare back. This time when he kissed her the pressure was stronger. She could feel his heart thudding heavily beneath her own, and although her own pulse remained steady, once again she quite enjoyed the kiss, found his touch quite pleasant.

His hands moved to her shoulders, and he raised his head to look down into her eyes. Then, as his gaze travelled downwards, she suddenly realised that she was only wearing her slip, and that one strap had come down, revealing a good portion of full cleavage.

Before she could make a move, he had reached down and pulled the strap back up, his hand brushing lightly over her breast. Then he retrieved the quilt and tucked it back up around her.

'You must be cold,' he said.

Nora was a little confused by now. She was the one who had made such an issue out of discouraging Mark, and here she was, lying half dressed in a strange house, letting him kiss her, even enjoying it. Maybe just the fact that there were no fireworks made that possible. But what kind of relationship was that?

Mark was an affectionate man, but obviously not a passionate one. If that had been Stephen, he would have been trying to get in the bed beside her by now. Instead, Mark had moved slightly away from her and was sitting with his feet planted on the floor, his long legs apart, his hands interlaced between them, staring down at the floor.

'Mark,' she said hesitantly. 'Is something wrong?'

He flashed her a quick smile. 'No. Nothing's wrong. I was just thinking about you, and wondering...'

'Wondering what?' she prompted.

'Well, about that picture in your bedroom. You know.'

'Oh,' she said blankly.

'I know it's none of my business, but was that the guy? I'm just curious. He must still be important to you if you keep his picture around.'

Nora gazed out of the window at the gathering dusk. If any man ever deserved the truth, this one did. She drew in a deep breath, raised her eyes and told him about Stephen's last unexpected appearance and his bland assumption that she would be thrilled to resume their relationship.

As she spoke, Mark's expression grew steadily blacker, until even before she'd finished his jaw was clamped shut, a little pulse throbbing there just under his ear, his brow thunderous, and his hands knotted together.

When she was through, there was a dead silence in the room for several long moments while he continued to stare down at his hands. Then he turned to her, still scowling, and banged a fist into his open palm.

'I'll kill the bastard,' he muttered angrily.

By now Nora was becoming seriously alarmed. 'Oh, there's no need for that,' she said lightly, trying to make a joke of it. 'By the time he left, he was definitely cowed and in no doubt that I meant what I said.' She reached out and put a hand over his. 'Mark, it's over. It was over even before I met you.'

Gradually, the tension began visibly to drain out of him. 'I just want to be certain,' he said in a milder tone. 'Surely you know how important you've become to me.'

She looked away. 'Yes, I know, but——'

He rose abruptly to his feet. 'Now. Are you hungry?'

She smiled up at him. 'Starved.'

After that first rather shaky introduction to the Leighton family, Nora's visit became more pleasant with each passing day. Once she grew accustomed to the informal, carefree atmosphere, she actually found it relaxing.

Mark was usually busy with his father overseeing the workings of the farm in the mornings, and she slept late, rising at nine o'clock or so to have a light late breakfast with Anna and her mother in the kitchen. When the men came in at one o'clock, the whole family gathered in the dining-room for an enormous meal. Then Mark would take Nora for a short walk around the farm, and she would rest again until dinner.

This leisurely life seemed to suit her. Both Leighton women were excellent cooks, and the bracing country air gave her a terrific appetite. By the end of the first week she already felt as though she'd gained five pounds, and her ankle was so much better that she was gradually able to discard the cane altogether.

That Saturday night, the whole family was invited to a party at a neighbouring farm, and Anna and her parents had talked about nothing else all morning. Although they automatically included Nora in their plans, as the day wore on she felt less and less enthusiastic about the enterprise.

That afternoon, on their usual walk after lunch, Nora and Mark had gone past the stables down a slight slope to a creek that ran through the property. When they reached the bank, he turned to her.

'Somehow I get the impression that you're less than thrilled about going to this party tonight,' he said. 'How about it? Do you really want to go?'

'The truth?' she asked with a smile.

'Nothing but,' he assured her.

'Well, then, unless it means a lot to you, I'd really rather not. I just don't feel quite up to meeting a lot of strangers just yet. But you go on with the others if you want to,' she added quickly. 'I won't mind a bit staying by myself.'

'I wouldn't hear of it,' he said firmly. 'In fact, an evening here by ourselves for a change sounds great to me. I'll make our excuses to the family. Are you ready to go back now?'

She nodded and they set off back to the house. As they walked, she glanced over at him from time to time. All during that week, she had found herself wondering off and on just why he had invited her in the first place, why he was being so kind and considerate. It didn't seem fair. He gave and she took. It was not the kind of relationship she was accustomed to. In fact, her past dealings with men had all been just the opposite.

After that first day in her room, he hadn't made one gesture or said one word that indicated any feeling on his part other than that of friendly interest. Although he was unfailingly attentive, he seemed to view her only as a person who needed his help, something like a stray dog. Of course, the almost constant presence of his family was a definite deterrent to any display of affection, but this didn't seem to bother him, and Nora began to wonder if she'd been mistaken about his feelings for her.

If so, she reasoned, it was probably for the best. For her part, she was simply basking contentedly in his friendship, enjoying it immensely. She felt as though she was being taken care of, even pampered, for the first time in her life. But why? What was in it for him?

As they passed by the stables, one of the men called out to Mark, beckoning him over. He stopped short and turned to her. 'Ben wants to speak to me. I'll just be a minute. It's cold out here. Do you want to go on ahead?'

'No, I'll wait for you.'

She watched him as he walked over to the stable door. He seemed so different here on the farm, in his own element, his rough clothes, his air of authority, as though he belonged here far more than he had in the city. He was standing there listening to Ben, his arms crossed over his chest, rubbing the side of his jaw thoughtfully, his face grave and attentive.

What a catch he would be for some lucky woman! At the thought, a wave of sadness passed over her. Why couldn't it be her? It was probably her own fault. She was the one who had discouraged him in the first place. But somehow that seemed to have changed.

He was walking back to her now, in long, firm strides, his hands tucked in the back pockets of his jeans. She could see his breath on the cold air, his dark hair ruffled by the breeze, and her heart caught in her throat. He was actually a downright handsome man, and she'd never even noticed!

'Problem all solved?' she asked, looking up at him.

He laughed shortly. 'It wasn't much of a problem.' He took her by the arm. 'Come on, let's get back to the house. It's freezing.'

Then, suddenly, he raised his head to look past her. His eyes lit up and he broke into a broad smile. 'Ah, I see the prodigal son has returned at last.' He raised a hand and called out. 'Tony, come and meet Nora.'

Nora turned around to see a slim, fair man walking across the veranda in front of the house, his step jaunty, his air confident. He was wearing a pair of dark trousers and a white turtle-necked sweater. His arms swung loosely at his sides, and he moved lightly, with a dancer's effortless grace.

As she watched him, Nora's eyes widened in horror and she clapped a hand to her mouth, stifling the cry of alarm that arose in her throat. There, walking down the path towards her, was a carbon copy of Stephen Kincaid.

CHAPTER SIX

FOR one shocked moment, Nora was half convinced it actually *was* Stephen. Through a trick of sunlight filtering through a tall oak tree just leafing out at the front of the house, Tony's face had been half hidden in the shadows.

Then as he came closer into the direct glare of the sun, she could see that although there was a superficial resemblance—the same general physical type, the same insouciant air—this was indeed a different man. In fact, his resemblance to his mother was startling, with her fair hair, pale blue eyes and slim frame.

With Mark's strong arm around her shoulders, his hard body pressed up against hers, there was nothing to be afraid of. He was introducing them now. She smiled and held out her hand.

'I'm glad to meet you at last, Tony,' she said. 'Mark has told me so much about you.'

He was eyeing her carefully, almost insolently, through half-closed lids, and another clang of alarm reverberated through her. She started to shrink back, but by now he had grasped her hand firmly in his. He kept it, and leaned down to kiss her cheek, his mouth lingering there just a few seconds more than was necessary.

'Well, Nora,' he said lazily, still holding her hand, 'it's nice to meet you, too.' His sharp gaze swept her up and down. 'Now I can see why poor old

Mark has talked about nothing else ever since he met you.'

Poor old Mark? She didn't like the sound of that. She frowned slightly and tugged at her hand. Finally he let it go, and clapped Mark on the back.

'She's everything you said she was, brother,' he said. 'You really got lucky this time.' He gave Nora another knowing look. 'A girl like you could convince even me to settle down.'

Fat chance, Nora thought. The type was so familiar to her it was almost laughable. Only this time there wasn't the slightest possibility she would be taken in by it. She glanced up at Mark. He was grinning broadly, gazing from one to the other, obviously delighted at Tony's hearty approval. Nora felt a slight twinge of annoyance. Didn't he know what the man was really like?

The rest of that day passed in a blur. Living so much on her own and with a rather rigidly disciplined life, Nora still couldn't quite get used to having so many people around nor so much hectic activity.

That day she was made doubly uncomfortable by having to go out of her way to avoid Tony, who seemed to be at her elbow every time she turned around, giving her those sly sideways glances that were so full of meaning.

As luck would have it, she was seated next to him at the dinner table that night, and although he made a point of leaning against her whenever he passed her something, since Mark was on her other side he had to be fairly circumspect about his attentions.

She couldn't help wondering why the come-on. She had no illusions that he found her irresistible.

What troubled her was that somehow he seemed able to recognise her own weakness for men like him. But that was all over. He was just the kind of man who had to prove his power to attract any woman that crossed his path, even one his own brother wanted.

Mark seemed to be so oblivious of what was going on that she was half angry at him. Like most naturally good people, he couldn't see evil in another person even when it came right out and hit him over the head. He obviously doted on his younger brother, even went out of his way to include him in his conversation with Nora.

As she watched the two men, only half listening to Tony's entertaining line of chatter, Nora felt a great surge of affection for Mark, for his solid presence, his generosity and dependability, and wondered how she ever could have fallen for men like Tony in the past. Thank heaven she was cured of that madness!

Just then she heard Tony speak her name. When she turned to him he searched her face, then fastened his eyes on hers in a direct look. After several long seconds, she was horrified to find she couldn't look away.

Finally he smiled, a mocking, knowing smile, just as though he were able to see into the depths of her soul. Nora felt downright violated by that look, her innermost self laid bare by those pale blue eyes. A shiver of fear ran up and down her spine. What had he seen in her to put that smile on his face?

Later that evening when the rest of the family had driven off to their party, Nora and Mark sat in the living-room by a roaring fire. Mark was in his usual chair, the evening paper on a table before him, leaning over and leafing through it. Luckily, Tony had a date of some kind and had left soon after dinner.

With Tony gone at last, Nora was able to relax, and she viewed the pleasant, homey scene with a sigh of contentment. She had come to love this room. Even though it was rather cluttered, crammed full of worn chintz furniture, with family photographs and mementoes covering every available surface, there was a feeling about it of grace and an easy informality that was very inviting.

A large grand piano stood in a dim corner of the huge room, but she'd never heard anyone play it. On an impulse, she got up from her chair and walked over to it. She lifted the lid and hit the keys with one hand in a soft, tentative chord.

'Do you play?' Mark called to her.

'Oh, I had the usual lessons as a child, but I haven't touched a piano for years.'

He got up and came over to her. 'Play something for me.'

She sat down on the bench and thought a moment, trying to recollect the pieces she used to know. Then she launched into a shaky rendition of 'The Jolly Farmer', ending up on a discordant note. She turned around, laughing at her clumsiness, and looked up at him, all primed for him to poke fun at her awful playing.

Instead, he was staring down at her intently, a serious expression on his face, his dark eyes narrowed at her and glittering in a look she hadn't seen there for a long time. He put his hands lightly on her shoulders and bent slowly towards her.

'Nora,' he said in a low, husky voice.

She waited breathlessly, her head in a whirl. Was this what she wanted? She liked this good, kind man enormously, even loved him in a way, but not in the way he deserved. She didn't know what to do. The one thing she *didn't* want to do was hurt him. And if she gave him any encouragement at all, that was exactly what she was afraid would happen.

His hands were moving on her shoulders now, kneading gently, his eyes never leaving hers. Then one hand moved to the back of her neck, his fingers threading up into her short dark hair, and he put his rough, bony cheek against hers. She could feel his warm breath on her face, feel the slow, laboured rise and fall of his chest against her back.

'Nora,' he murmured again, more urgently this time.

She twisted her head around to look up at him, and before she could say anything his mouth was on hers, so soft, so gentle, his lips moving against hers in a slow, sensuous rhythm that made no demands, but which was anything but friendly. Her lips parted instinctively, and the pressure of his mouth increased. One hand slipped around her neck to move slowly downwards.

Then, suddenly, he sank down on the bench beside her, facing away from her. He crossed one arm in front of her, bracing his hand flat on the bench, and raised the other to her cheek.

'I think you know how I feel about you, Nora,' he said.

'Mark, I don't know what to say,' she faltered.

He put a finger on her lips. 'I know. And I promised I wouldn't push.' He gazed directly into her eyes, a long, penetrating look. 'But can you honestly say you felt nothing just now when I kissed you?'

She rose to her feet, skirted around the piano bench, and started pacing back and forth, stopping some distance away from him. Finally she turned around to face him.

'No,' she said slowly. 'I can't say that. Of course I felt something.' She spread her hands wide. 'But not what I think you want me to feel.' She laughed shortly. 'I don't think I'm *able* to feel that way any more, don't dare *allow* myself to! I don't want to hurt you. You've been so good to me. I'm only thinking of you. It wouldn't be fair to you to lie, to tell you that I feel something that just isn't there. You deserve much better than that.'

He rose up slowly and came walking towards her, smiling crookedly. 'Why don't you let me be the judge of that?' He put his hands on her shoulders and gazed down at her with smouldering eyes. 'I love you, Nora,' he said in a voice of dead seriousness. 'I want to marry you.'

She stared up at him. She'd never dreamed it had gone that far. She had assumed he was like all the rest, that what he had in mind was a brief affair, then they would go their separate ways. She was utterly speechless.

'Well?' he said after a long, tense moment. 'Don't you have anything to say to that?'

She gazed down at her feet, biting her lip, her thoughts in an utter turmoil. The one thing that was utterly clear to her, however, was that marriage to a man she didn't desire was out of the question. She had to tell him the truth. It was better to wound his pride a little bit now than to really hurt him later on.

Finally she looked up at him again. 'Mark,' she said slowly. 'I value your friendship more than I can say, and I don't want to lose it. How can I convince you that I'm not the one for you, that I'm through with all that? There are probably a thousand women out there just panting for a chance at a man like you. Why me?'

He shrugged his broad shoulders. 'I don't know. Love is a mystery, isn't it? I only know that the minute I saw you I wanted you. Any way I could get you,' he added grimly. 'Short of abducting you physically—and don't think I wasn't tempted.' He reached out to take her hand in his, turning it over and over. 'I think you could learn to love me if you gave yourself half a chance.'

'I do love you, Mark. I just don't——'

He raised a hand. 'I know. No gongs clang. No drums roll. Well, maybe in time they will.'

'It just wouldn't be fair to you...'

'Look, I know you don't care for me in a romantic way.' He shrugged. 'I guess I'm not a very romantic guy. You've said you were through with all that anyway. I believe you meant it. Then let me ask you what you're going to do with the rest of your life. Are you going to spend it alone, in a job you don't even like? I'm thirty-eight years old. I've had my share of experimenting with what passes for love these days, and I'm tired of it. I'm well set up in life. I can offer you security, a good home, children. I may not be your idea of a dashing hero, but I think I could make you happy. Unless I'm actually repulsive to you...'

'No, of course not. You know very well it's not that.'

'Well, then? Why not think it over? I won't press you again. All I ask is that you think about it.'

Why? That was the question that kept running through her mind as she lay in bed later that night, tossing and turning, too worked up to go to sleep. Here was a man who could probably have any woman he wanted, a proud man, yet he had humbled himself before her. She'd be crazy to let him go. He knew how she felt—or *didn't* feel! And he was far from repulsive to her.

In fact, she had come to enjoy the warmth of his touch, his embraces, and she *had* responded to those few brief kisses more than she'd admitted to him, or to herself. Wasn't that enough?

She was weakening, she knew it. She *did* love him. And he was right. There was nothing else she really wanted. To marry a man like Mark, to share his life, come to live with such a fine, loving family in this wonderful haven of peace and contentment— what more could she ask?

Certainly she'd never experienced that kind of warmth and love with her own family. She thought about her long-suffering mother, who for years had put up with a philandering husband; her own father, with such poor grace, substituting expensive clothes, trips, an exciting social whirl for the fidelity and love he couldn't give her. Mark's family was so different, their values so much more solid and enduring.

She could be a part of all that. As for worrying about Mark, he was a grown man who'd said himself he'd had all the experience he wanted with amorous adventures, and as she finally drifted off to sleep she had already half made up her mind to accept his proposal.

The next morning was grey and overcast. After breakfast, Mark and Nora decided to take a walk before it started to rain. It was Sunday, and the rest of the family had gone off to church, presumably including Tony, since he was nowhere around.

'What do you think of Tony?' Mark asked her as they strolled along slowly, hand in hand, towards the small stream that ran along some distance behind the stables.

She gave him a swift glance. 'He's everything you said he was,' she assured him. 'And more,' she added drily.

'He was quite taken with you, too.' He stopped and turned to her. 'I'm not a particularly demonstrative man, but I want you to know that you and Tony are probably the two people who mean the most to me in the world. I want you to be friends.'

She cocked her head to one side and looked up at him. 'Whoever told you you weren't demonstrative?' she asked. 'I haven't found that to be true at all.'

'Ah, but that's only with you,' he said with a smile. 'I love you.' His face sobered. 'And I don't love lightly or often.'

Something in his expression chilled her. She was reminded of the near-murderous jealousy he had displayed over Stephen. She'd almost forgotten about that. Was it going to be a problem? She shivered a little, and he put his arm around her.

'Are you cold? Should we go in?'

'A little,' she said hurriedly. 'It is getting a little chilly. I probably should have brought a sweater along.'

He glanced up at the leaden sky as a few fat drops of rain began to fall. 'We'd better go back. It's going to start pouring any minute.'

By the time they reached the house, the rain was coming down in earnest, and they had to run the last several feet to keep from getting soaked. When they reached the shelter of the porch, Ben, the head groom from the stable, was standing there waiting for them.

'You'd better come down with me and take a look at Lightning, boss,' he said to Mark. 'His leg looks worse.'

Mark frowned. 'Have you called the vet?'

The other man nodded. 'Yeah, but it's Sunday, remember. He's already gone off to church.'

Mark turned to Nora. 'I'll have to go. Lightning is our prize stud. I'll be back as soon as the vet shows up.'

'Of course,' Nora said. 'You go on.'

The two men turned and ran out into the yard down to the stables through the downpour. Nora looked after them for a moment, worrying that Mark wasn't wearing a raincoat or hat. Then she had to smile at the domestic turn her thoughts were taking. She turned and went inside the house. If domesticity had become her bent, she could use it by washing up the breakfast dishes instead of fussing over Mark.

She went into the kitchen and began clearing the table. It was cosy in the warm room, the rain slashing against the window-pane, and she hummed a little under her breath as she ran hot water into the sink. After the nocturnal battle she'd had with herself in bed last night, she'd awakened that morning half convinced she really might marry him.

She'd finished washing the dishes and was just rummaging through a drawer looking for a clean dish-towel when she heard the front door open and close and footsteps coming towards the kitchen. Already smiling, she turned around to greet Mark.

Instead, there, standing in the doorway, was Tony. Nora's smile faded. He was leaning against the frame in a typical graceful slouch, the same mocking grin on his face, eyeing her lazily.

'What are you doing here?' she blurted out. 'I thought you'd gone to church with the others.'

He raised one eyebrow and chuckled deep in his throat. 'Who, me? As a matter of fact, I just got up.'

He pushed himself away from the doorway, stretched widely and came walking slowly towards her, his eyes never leaving hers. He stopped only inches away from her. He was several inches shorter than Mark, and their eyes were almost on a level.

'Well,' he said with satisfaction. 'We're alone at last.'

Nora turned her head quickly and reached into the open drawer behind her. 'Right,' she said, pulling out a towel and handing it to him. 'You're just in time to dry the dishes.'

He took it from her without a word and draped it around his neck. Then he raised a hand towards her, and she shrank back immediately, terrified he was going to touch her. Instead, he reached past her, took out a plate from the dish rack on the sink, and started drying it slowly.

'Why so jumpy, Nora?' he asked, widening his blue eyes innocently. 'I won't hurt you.'

She laughed nervously and walked away from him towards the table in the centre of the room. 'I never imagined you would,' she said, keeping her voice steady. She glanced back at him over her shoulder. 'Or could,' she added, eyeing him carefully.

'Ah,' he said. 'The kitten has claws.'

They worked in silence for some time, the rain still pattering down outside. Nora's heart was thudding. She hated being alone with Tony in the silent, empty house. She kept telling herself she had nothing to fear from him. He meant her no harm. It was just his nature to try to charm every woman he met. Still, she avoided looking at him or speaking to him, and only hoped Mark would come back soon.

When he'd finished drying the dishes, he hung the towel up neatly on the rack to dry. Then he leaned back against the counter, took a cigarette out of the package in his shirt pocket and lit it. He folded his arms in front of him and gazed at her through half-shut eyes, the smoke drifting up around his head.

She had just cleaned off the crumbs from the tablecloth and started to fold it carefully when she heard him speaking to her. 'So, tell me,' he drawled. 'Are you going to marry old Mark?'

Without even glancing his way, she continued folding the cloth. 'That's not really your affair, is it?' she said shortly. Then she couldn't help herself.

She raised her head and glared at him. 'Why do you call him "old" Mark? It's so—condescending.'

He shrugged. 'I don't know. Don't you think it suits him? You know, the Rock of Gibraltar, the one we all depend on. Great stuff, but——' He took one last puff then ground out his cigarette in a clean saucer he had just dried. 'But rather boring, don't you think?'

'That doesn't even deserve an answer,' she said in a low voice throbbing with contempt. 'Who are you to judge him?'

'Oh, I'd never judge old Mark.' He started to walk towards her. 'It's you I have reservations about.'

She gave him a swift look. 'What do you mean? I think Mark is the finest man I've ever met, and I like him enormously.'

'Sure,' he said. 'Everybody does. But a man like Mark can't possibly satisfy a woman like you.'

'Oh, and I suppose you think you could,' she said in disgust. 'How can you talk that way about your own brother?'

'Oh, all old Mark really cares about are his horses,' he said in that same maddening drawl. 'And you're not married to him, after all. Not even engaged.'

She couldn't argue with that, so she only ignored him. He was so close to her now that she could see the light stubble on his jaw, a few strands of fair hair falling over his forehead. He had that same intense, cynical look in his eyes that she'd seen before—in Stephen, in her own father—a look she had come to detest.

The next thing she knew his hands were around her neck, his face bent close to hers. She started to cry out, but his mouth was already covering hers, his tongue seeking against her lips. To her utter horror, by some strange, unfathomable metamorphosis, she could feel her anger gradually, insidiously turning into desire.

Her head whirled crazily. Mark was forgotten completely. She could feel the urgency in Tony, in the way his slim, hard body pressed against hers so insistently, and a familiar thrill of excitement, of danger, coursed through her.

What was going on here? She despised this man, and all men like him. How could it be that one of them could still wield this kind of power over her? She loved Mark. Mark! The thought of him brought her to her senses at last.

She wrenched her mouth away, put her hands flat against Tony's chest and with all her strength pushed at him so hard that he almost fell backwards. She stood there trembling with rage, wiping her mouth with the back of her hand where his lips had been.

'Don't you ever come near me again!' she said in a low voice still throbbing with emotion. 'Or I'll tell Mark just what his darling brother is up to behind his back.'

Recovered by now, Tony was smiling again and shaking his head slowly from side to side. 'I don't think so,' he said confidently. 'Not if you really do love him.' Then the smile faded. 'I was right about you. Admit it. You wanted it as much as I did.'

Just then she heard the front door open and close. It must be Mark. Before going to him, she gave Tony one last look. 'Don't count on that, Tony,' she said in a warning tone. 'I'm not the easy mark you think I am.'

'Ah, but Nora,' he said easily, 'that only whets my appetite even more.'

She turned quickly on her heel and stalked out of the room.

All that day the ugly scene haunted Nora. Even though she had ended it practically before it had begun, still she couldn't quite forget that for just a moment she had responded to Tony's kiss, and she despised herself for it.

Somehow from the moment she'd first laid eyes on him she'd known, deep in the recesses of her unconscious mind, that he was dangerous to her, not because of anything he could do to harm her or her relationship with Mark, but because of her own weakness. Now she felt just as though she had actually betrayed Mark, a man who loved her, trusted her. How could she live with that?

As upsetting as it was, however, it had actually accomplished one thing of value. It had brought an end to Tony's suggestive looks and innuendoes. He left her alone for the rest of the day, at least, and if Mark noticed that she and Tony were avoiding each other he didn't say anything about it.

She was finally able to convince herself that at most it was an unpleasant episode, unimportant in itself, and certainly never to be repeated. All she had to do was stay out of his way. Then, that night at dinner, to her great relief, he announced that he'd be leaving in the morning on another business trip.

As she lay alone in bed that night, however, she couldn't quite get the image of Tony's mocking smile out of her mind, and her blood ran cold at the memory. She'd reacted to him just as she had in the past to similar men, men like Stephen, and it all came back to her now—the excitement, the uncertainty, the risk, the anxiety. Once she had actually found all that thrilling.

Mark, with his steady love, had never aroused those feelings in her. He had said it himself. No bells clanged, no drums rolled at his restrained lovemaking, perhaps partly because he was so obviously holding back, keeping his own desire in check.

She turned over on her stomach and buried her head in the pillow. So what if Mark didn't excite her? She did love him in her way, and if she married him she'd be safe from men like Tony.

She finally fell into a fitful sleep, with the most important question of all still unanswered. How could she possibly agree to marry Mark if his brother could wield that kind of power over her?

The next day, Mark and his father had to travel into town for a horse auction. They were to leave right after breakfast. Apparently Tony had gone already to catch an early plane.

'You're invited to come along to the auction with us, Nora,' Mark said as he finished up his bacon and eggs. 'But I'm afraid you might find it tiring.'

'And extremely boring!' Anna put in. She turned to Nora. 'Don't let him talk you into going,' she said firmly. 'All he'll be interested in is the horses and you'll be left to shift for yourself out in the cold.'

Nora laughed. 'I'll take your word for it. Sorry, Mark, your sister talked me out of it.'

The two men left soon after, taking along Mrs Leighton to drop her off at a friend's house. When they were gone, Anna got up from the table and went over to the stove.

'How about another cup of coffee, Nora?'

'Yes, please.' She half rose out of her chair. 'But please quit waiting on me. I won't be fit for anything when I get back home, you've all spoiled me so rotten.'

Anna came back with the coffee-pot and refilled their mugs. 'It's been a pleasure,' she assured her warmly. She sat down and took a sip of coffee. 'I've never seen Mark so happy. He's like a young boy again.'

Nora gave the other woman a guilty look. She didn't want to get into a discussion of her relationship with Mark just now. But Anna was leaning back comfortably in her chair, staring off into space, her expression bland. Apparently she was only making polite conversation and didn't expect any kind of response.

As she watched her, Nora was struck once again by the strong resemblance to her brother. She was a handsome woman, with her solid bone structure and casually knotted hair, not beautiful or even pretty, but with a certain dignity and authority about her that inspired admiration and respect, just like Mark. She was only a few years younger than Mark, somewhere in her mid-thirties, and Nora was suddenly curious about her.

'Anna,' she said, 'can I ask you a personal question?'

'Sure. Go ahead.'

'It's none of my business, but I can't help wondering why you've never married.'

Anna raised her dark eyebrows. 'Oh, but I was married. He was killed five years ago in a bad fall from a horse.'

'Oh, I'm sorry.' She thought a moment. 'But that was five years ago.'

'You mean why haven't I married again?'

Nora nodded. 'Yes. You're a very attractive woman.'

'Well,' Anna replied, 'we're a rather peculiar family. We don't fall often, but when we do it's forever.' She laughed. 'Always excepting Tony, of course. But then, Tony is in a class by himself,' she added drily.

'Forever is a long time,' Nora said softly.

'Well, let's just say I've never met a man who could match Robert.' She shrugged. 'Besides, Mother hasn't been well for the past few years, and Dad and the boys need me here.'

'Tell me about Tony,' Nora said. 'Mark claims he's the brains of the family. In fact, from the way he describes him, he sounds like some kind of paragon of all the virtues.'

Anna picked up her empty mug and carried it to the sink. 'Don't you believe it,' she called over her shoulder. 'That's just Mark's modesty talking. I love Tony, don't misunderstand. He's extremely clever, well-educated, and can be a great charmer when he wants to. But for my money Mark's got him beat in every department.' She turned around and gave Nora a sober look. 'That's why I'm so glad he's found you. If any man deserves happiness, it's Mark.'

Just then there was the sound of a car coming up the drive, the squeal of tyres, a door slamming. Anna peered out of the kitchen window and made a face.

'Oh, drat, we've got company.'

Nora started to get out of her chair. 'I have some things to do in my room. You'll want to visit.'

'Oh, please stay. It's only one of our neighbours. You're bound to meet her sooner or later anyway. The word must have got around that you're staying here as Mark's guest. She's had her cap set on him for years, and it was only a matter of time before she came around to give you the once-over. She won't stay long.'

There came a sharp rap on the front door, then the sound of it opening and shutting and heels tapping across the hall towards the kitchen.

'Anna?' a woman's voice called out. 'Are you home?'

Even before she appeared at the doorway, Nora knew who the voice belonged to. She wasn't surprised, then, when the blonde woman they'd run into the first night she'd had dinner with Mark back in September came barging into the room.

'Hello, Sylvia,' Anna said in a resigned tone. She turned to Nora. 'Nora, this is Sylvia Armstrong, a neighbour of ours.'

CHAPTER SEVEN

SYLVIA glanced over at Nora and gave her a surprisingly pleasant smile. 'Hello, Nora. I believe we met before one evening several months ago in Washington. Mark told me later you were helping him resolve his tax problems.'

'Yes,' Nora replied. 'That's right.'

'Sit down, Sylvia,' Anna said. 'I'll pour you a cup of coffee. Or are you in a hurry?'

'Thanks, Anna. No, I'm in no rush.' She took the chair next to Nora. 'I've always been helpless with figures,' she said with a little laugh. 'You must be very clever to have such a responsible job.'

An olive branch? Nora smiled. 'Not really. It's a knack, something one is born with.'

'I hear you had an accident,' Sylvia went on. 'Was it serious?'

'Oh, no. Just a sprain. It's all healed now, thanks to the Leighton family.' Nora wondered how much Sylvia knew about the actual circumstances. 'Mark just happened to be there when the car hit me and kindly offered me sanctuary here while I recuperated.'

'I see. And how long will you be staying?'

'Here, Sylvia,' Anna broke in. She set the cup down on the table and shoved it towards her quite firmly. 'Here's your coffee.' She sat down, gave Nora a reassuring smile, then turned to Sylvia. 'Nora is going to stay as long as she needs to—or wants to,' she stated in a no-nonsense tone of voice. 'We're enjoying her visit too much to let her go just yet.'

'Of course,' Sylvia murmured. She took a sip of coffee. 'Has Mark gone to the horse auction?'

'Yes,' Anna replied. 'He's got his eye on that chestnut colt of Foley's.'

'Do you ride, Nora?' Sylvia asked, turning to her.

'Horses?' Nora shook her head. 'No, I'm afraid not.'

'Nora's a city girl,' Anna put in kindly. 'Give her time and she'll learn.' She nodded at Nora as though for corroboration.

Nora laughed. 'I'm not so sure about that.'

'Well, they do say it's never too late to learn.' Sylvia smiled at her, then turned to Anna. 'Has the roan mare foaled yet?'

The two women launched into an esoteric technical discussion of horseflesh that was totally over Nora's head. She watched them, listening with only half an ear and feeling like a being from another planet for all the sense their conversation made to her.

They were very much alike, not physically, but in interests, in the way they wore their expensive, casual clothes, a certain air of self-assurance about them. Both were obviously country women, with that aura of blooming good health that came from spending a lot of time out of doors.

She had expected to dislike Sylvia, at least to have to contend with some hostility from her. After all, she herself was the interloper, only here at all as Mark's guest. She couldn't quite forget that scene

in the restaurant, the possessive way Sylvia's hand
had rested on Mark's arm, or the warning look she
had given her.

But that had been in the city. Now, here in the
country, the blonde was on her own territory, and
she seemed much more relaxed, even anxious to put
Nora at ease and make her feel welcome. After an
hour of pleasant conversation, Nora found her quite
friendly and only mildly curious about her status
in the Leighton household.

In fact, when Nora told her how she'd first met
Mark, the day he'd stormed into her office demanding an explanation of her letter threatening to
audit his books, she laughed in genuine amusement.

'I can just see Mark, can't you Anna?' she said.
'He's the mildest of men most of the time, but when
a moral principle is involved he turns into an
avenging angel. Remember, Anna, the time he beat
Tom Conway senseless for mistreating one of the
horses?'

As Nora gradually warmed to the blonde, she
couldn't help wondering why Sylvia and Mark
hadn't married long ago. Was she one of the past
adventures he'd mentioned? They had everything
in common. She obviously adored him. The way
her eyes lit up and her voice softened whenever his
name was mentioned was a dead giveaway.

Just then there came the sound of another car
coming up the driveway. Anna rose up out of her
seat, went over to the window, pulled aside the
curtain and peered out.

'It's Mark,' she said. 'I wonder what he's doing
back so early. And he's alone.' She turned around

slowly, a troubled look on her face. 'Something must have happened.'

She ran out into the front hall, and in a moment there came the sound of voices, Mark's low and rumbling, Anna's pitched high in sudden dismay. In a moment she appeared back at the kitchen door, her face drawn and drained of colour.

'It's Mother,' she said in a tight voice. 'They've taken her to the hospital. I've got to go to her.' Mark had come up to stand behind her, his hands on her shoulders, steadying her. She whirled around and looked up at him. 'Mark, you've got to take me.'

'All right,' he said quietly. 'Whenever you're ready.'

'I'll just go get a coat.'

Nora and Sylvia had risen from their chairs and were standing there, staring helplessly at Mark. His face was set and grim, his jaws clamped tightly together.

Sylvia went over to him. 'Mark, is there anything I can do?'

He shook his head slowly, as though in a daze. 'No,' he said. 'I don't think so.' He glanced at Nora, then back to Sylvia again. 'It's her heart. We'd just dropped her off at the Taylor farm down the road, and she simply collapsed. We rushed her right to the hospital. Dad's with her now.' He walked over to Nora. 'I'll have to go back to take Anna.'

'I can do that if you like,' Sylvia said.

Mark gave her a blank look, then shook his head. 'No. I have to be there, in case . . .' His voice trailed off.

Nora put a hand on his arm. 'Of course you do, Mark. Would you like me to come with you, or should I stay here in case you need something?'

He put his hand over hers and smiled at her. 'You might as well stay here. There's nothing you can do there, and it could be a long wait until we find out how serious it is. They're talking about emergency coronary bypass surgery. Will you be all right here on your own?'

'Of course. You and Anna go on ahead. Please call me when you have some news.'

'If you don't mind, Mark,' Sylvia said, 'I'd like to come along. I have my car, and you might need it.'

Mark nodded absently. 'If you like.'

Anna appeared then, struggling into her heavy jacket, and the three of them went outside. Nora stood at the door watching them as they drove off, then closed it and walked slowly back into the kitchen. It was eleven o'clock. At least she could make herself useful, perhaps think about making lunch.

During the next few days, there was either constant activity at the farm, with neighbours and friends coming and going, or Nora was left entirely on her own. She had come to take over virtually all the household chores so that Anna would be free to spend as much time as possible with her mother, and she was grateful to have something to do during the long hours alone.

Finally, on Wednesday, Mrs Leighton was pronounced out of danger and in a stable condition. She'd had the bypass surgery and come through it beautifully. Mark and his father and Anna had set off for the hospital right after breakfast that morning to visit her, and while they were gone Nora cleaned the kitchen and did the dishes as usual, then wandered aimlessly through the house.

It had come to seem so empty with the others gone so much, even vaguely depressing. All of a sudden she realised why.

She didn't belong here. Her life was in Washington. She thought of her own apartment, even her job, with an unexpected wave of nostalgia. They weren't much, but they were hers. And as for her disappointment at not getting the job she'd expected, there would be other opportunities for advancement in the future.

But what was she going to do about Mark? Somehow, after seeing him with Sylvia, she couldn't help noticing how the blonde woman fitted into the family so effortlessly, and she was more than ever convinced she couldn't marry him. Even he must realise that now.

Mark and his father returned early, since Mrs Leighton wasn't allowed visitors for long. Anna and Sylvia had stayed on with her, and Sylvia would drive Anna home later.

After lunch, Mark scraped his chair back from the table and rose to his feet. 'How about a walk, Nora?' he asked.

With all the confusion about his mother's illness, they had dropped their habit of walking together after lunch. She looked at him. Now that his mother was out of danger, he seemed more like his old self again. The haggard look was gone, and his old air of quiet confidence was back.

'I should get the kitchen cleaned up,' she said hesitantly.

'Listen, you've been chief cook and bottle washer around here long enough. You came here for a rest, remember?'

'Well, all right. I'd enjoy a short walk.'

As she put on her boots and heavy jacket and tied a scarf around her head, she decided that now would be a good time to tell him what was on her mind. She hadn't wanted to bother him with her problems while he had still been so concerned about his mother, but, since that load was lifted now, she might as well get it over with.

They went outside into the cold, crisp air. The sun was shining, but since the temperature was near freezing it didn't cast much warmth. Nora put on her gloves, and they set off towards the stables. As they went, she tried to think of how to tell him, and finally decided the best way was just to come right out with it.

When they came to the stables, she stopped and turned to him. 'Mark,' she said. He looked down at her. 'I think it's time for me to go home.'

His eyes widened. 'Home? You mean back to Washington?'

She nodded.

'But why?'

'I just think it's best.' They started walking slowly again. 'The last thing Anna needs is a guest on her hands, with your mother in the hospital. And besides . . .' She hesitated.

'Besides, what?'

'Well, I only took a two-week leave, and I left the apartment in such a mess it will take me days to get it in shape. And I should see the doctor again for that physical I promised him.' She smiled. 'Although you've treated me so well here I don't think I really need one any more.'

'I don't want you to go,' he said. 'I thought you'd been enjoying yourself.'

'Oh, I have been, immensely. But you have other things on your mind now. And there's no reason for you to drive me all the way back to Washington,' she added quickly. 'I'm sure there's a bus I can take.'

'No,' he said curtly. 'I'll drive you if you really are determined to go.'

'I think it's best, Mark,' she said softly.

'When do you want to leave?'

'Well, if you're really going to insist on taking me, we should probably get an early start in the morning.'

'So soon?'

'Yes.'

He didn't say anything for a while. He raised his head and squinted up at the sky, his breath frosty on the cold air, and as she watched him a pang of real regret pierced her heart. He was such a wonderful man. She knew she'd hurt him, and she searched for a way to soften the blow of her decision to leave.

After a moment, he turned to her and took her arm. 'We'd better keep going or we'll freeze to death.'

They continued walking on in silence until they arrived at the creek. They stopped again and stood looking down at the rushing stream. The cold, clear water was in full flood from the melting snow in the mountains, and the flat rocks at the bottom on the bed were clearly visible.

'I've enjoyed getting to know Sylvia,' she said at last. 'She's very nice. Attractive, too.'

'Yes,' he said. 'I suppose so.'

'I'm surprised you and she haven't formed a closer relationship through the years,' she went on in a casual tone. 'You have so much in common, and she certainly seems to think very highly of you.' She laughed. 'But maybe you already have.'

He turned to her, both eyebrows raised. 'Have what?'

She shrugged. 'You know. Become romantically involved.'

He laughed shortly. 'I don't know about Sylvia, but that thought never crossed my mind. We're probably too much alike, and have known each other too long for anything like that.' He put his hands on her shoulders and turned her around to face him. He stared down at her, smiling warmly, his dark eyes glinting. 'Besides, you know what I want.'

'Mark,' she began, and turned her head away.

'Nora, look at me.' He put a hand on her face and forced her head around. 'I told you I wouldn't pressure you,' he said softly. 'But you're going to have to make up your mind sooner or later. I'm a patient man, but I have my limits.'

'Mark, I value your friendship so much——'

'That isn't what I want,' he broke in impatiently. 'It's got to be one way or the other.'

Nora's mind raced. She dreaded the thought of giving him up entirely, but what else could she do? She simply didn't love him in the way he wanted, the way he deserved to be loved. At that moment, she was so strongly tempted to agree to marry him she was afraid she might actually blurt it out. And then spend the rest of her life regretting it. Still, to lose him altogether was unthinkable.

'Are you giving me an ultimatum, Mark?' she asked at last.

He pursed his lips thoughtfully. 'I guess maybe I am.' His hands tightened on her shoulders, and his eyes burned into hers. 'I love you, Nora. I want to marry you. It's no good trying to throw Sylvia at me. If I'd wanted Sylvia, I would have done something about it years ago, long before I met you.'

She still couldn't make up her mind. 'I need more time,' she said. 'If you press me today, I'd have to say no.' She raised a hand and placed it on his cheek. 'Not because I don't love you. I do, in my way. But I'm afraid you want more from me, expect more from me, than I'd ever be able to give.'

'All right,' he said. 'I can wait a while longer. But please don't go back to Washington just yet. I want you to finish out your visit.' He paused. 'I really need you now, Nora, more than ever. In the meantime I won't say another word, and by the weekend, if you still want to go home, I'll take you. And if you still haven't made up your mind to marry me, I won't call you or try to see you for a time, but eventually I'll come to you and I'll want an answer. It has to be one way or the other.'

'All right,' she said. 'That sounds fair enough. I'll stay until Sunday, and I think I can promise you an answer by then.'

* * *

During the next few days, Nora see-sawed back and forth, trying to analyse her feelings, and by Friday afternoon she was no closer to a decision than before. She'd be leaving on Sunday, and she still had no idea what she would say to him.

The whole family had gone to the hospital that morning to visit Mrs Leighton, who was recovering nicely from open heart surgery, and Nora was alone in the house, in the kitchen, making herself a sandwich for lunch.

What did she really want? What was the right thing to do? She had asked herself these questions over and over again, ever since their talk on Wednesday. Now time was fast running out. Only two more days, and she'd promised Mark she'd have an answer for him.

She wished she had someone to confide in, someone to advise her. It was ironic that the only person she could think of she would trust to help her make a decision on such an important issue was Mark himself.

Well, she argued as she carried her solitary lunch into the small den and turned on the television, didn't that tell her something? There was a game-show on, and she turned off the sound, staring blankly at the flickering shapes as they cavorted mindlessly around on the screen. If Mark Leighton was the one person in the world she trusted implicitly, why not spend the rest of her life with him?

'Because I don't love him,' she muttered aloud.

But I *do* love him, she added silently. Then what am I worried about? Just marry him and hope for the best? He was right. He could offer her devotion, a steady, dependable love, fidelity, a home, children, all the things she really longed for. But wasn't that just it? He could give her everything, but what did she have to give him? It was the fear that she would only be using him to gratify her own needs that tormented her.

The next morning Nora awoke at her usual time to a strangely silent house. Usually there were voices coming from the kitchen at that hour of the morning. She glanced at the bedside clock. It was eight-thirty. Perhaps they'd gone early to the hospital.

She rolled over on her back and gazed out of the window at another sunny day. The landscape was still wintry, the branches of the trees bare and brown, but even the pale January sun was better than the snow and slush she'd left behind in Washington.

As usual, her thoughts turned immediately to the decision she had to make about Mark's proposal. Somehow she still hoped that a blinding flash of insight would miraculously appear after a good night's sleep, but she felt no nearer a decision now than she had on any other morning.

She got out of bed and stumbled into the bathroom to shower. Then she got dressed in grey woollen trousers and white silk blouse, brushed out her short dark hair and went down the hall to the kitchen. She rather enjoyed having the house to herself so much these days. It was a lovely old place, and she'd hate to leave it.

In the kitchen there was juice in the fridge and coffee on the stove. She wasn't particularly hungry, and a piece of toast was all the breakfast she needed, considering the huge midday meals the family always had.

When she'd finished her second cup of coffee, she wandered out into the entry hall and started to climb the stairs. Mark's mother was due to come home this afternoon, and she'd promised Anna she'd change the sheets on her bed.

Since her own guest room was on the ground floor, she'd only been on the second landing once, briefly, yesterday, when Anna had taken her to the bedroom her parents shared and showed her the linen cupboard where the fresh sheets were kept.

After she'd finished stripping the bed and re-making it carefully, she decided to look around a little. The family wouldn't mind, and she was curious to see if all the rooms up here were as spacious and comfortably furnished as the rest of the house.

Presumably all the bedrooms were up here, and it wasn't until she'd poked her head in one that was obviously Anna's and another that seemed to be another guest room that she admitted to herself the real reason for her exploration. She wanted to see Mark's room. Why? What did she hope to find there? Possibly a clue to the man himself?

In any case she finally came to a bedroom that had to be his. Through the open door she saw a wide bed, neatly made, covered with a dark red tailored spread that looked very masculine, and lying on top was a heavy sheepskin jacket that she recognised as his. There were matching draperies at the window, pictures of horses on the walls, and

over against the far wall a tall glass-fronted case
that seemed to be full of trophies of some kind.

She stepped inside and went over to the case for
a closer look. There must have been twenty or more
gold and silver cups, all for different athletic events,
and all with the name, Mark Leighton, engraved
on them. Track, swimming, football, basketball,
baseball, every sport one could imagine, were all
represented, both from high school and college.

There were also a few framed photographs set
on top of the case. Mark as a young boy, dressed
in riding clothes and sitting astride an enormous
black horse. Tony and Mark together, each holding
up a string of fish, Tony grinning impudently and
Mark with his characteristic sweet, rather inward
smile. A football team with Mark standing tall in
the last row.

She was so fascinated by this impressive record
of his past triumphs that when she heard a sudden
noise behind her, footsteps coming down the hall,
she didn't even have time to collect her thoughts,
much less think who it could be, until she heard
his voice.

'I see you've discovered the vestiges of my mis-
spent youth.'

She straightened up and whirled around, mor-
tified to have been caught snooping. 'Oh, Mark,
I'm sorry. I shouldn't have intruded like this. I came
up to change your mother's bed, and then couldn't
resist the temptation——' She broke off with a
helpless shrug. 'I thought you'd already gone to
the hospital with the others.'

But he didn't look in the least angry. In fact, he
looked like a different man altogether, a man she'd

never seen before, and she could only stand there and stare at him. He'd obviously just bathed and dressed. His chest and shoulders were bare, his hair tousled and falling over his forehead, and as he came walking towards her he was slowly buckling the belt of his dark trousers.

'No need to apologise,' he said with a smile. He made a gesture of dismissal towards the caseful of trophies. 'I don't know why I still hang on to those things. Sentiment, I guess.'

She hardly heard what he was saying. He was so close to her now that she could see the spot on his jaw his razor had missed and smell the soap he'd used. His hair was still slightly damp, and a few drops of water still clung to his skin. But most of all, what riveted her attention was his magnificent physique.

She'd always known, of course, that he was a powerfully built man, strongly muscled, with wide shoulders and a broad chest. But now, seeing his upper body bare for the first time, she was awestruck by his sheer physical beauty. There wasn't an ounce of fat on him. His chest was smooth except for a narrow trail of coarse black hair that tapered down and disappeared under the low-slung trousers.

She raised her head to see that he was staring at her, a slightly puzzled look on his face. Then, slowly, he walked over to the wardrobe. He reached inside, pulled out a fresh white shirt and slid his arms inside the sleeves.

Watching him, each slow, careful gesture, Nora was stunned into speechless immobility. Why had she never appreciated the powerful physical attraction of the man, with his square jaw, long, straight nose and liquid dark brown eyes? The image flashed through her mind of the slim, fair men she had always thought of as 'her type', and she wondered how she could ever have harboured such a silly notion.

He was walking back towards her now. She waited, hardly daring to breathe. He stopped a few feet away and looked down at her.

'You look pretty perky this morning,' he said in a low voice. 'Even more beautiful without make-up.'

'Thank you,' she said in a shaky voice. She smiled. 'You look pretty good yourself.' She put a hand nervously at her throat. 'Are you hungry? I could fix you some breakfast.'

'No,' he said. 'Not just yet.' In one short step he covered the distance between them and gazed down at her, his expression sober, dead serious. 'I was hoping that you might have come to give me an answer.'

She raised her eyes to his, searching them, as though trying to penetrate beyond them to what was in his mind. Did she dare trust him? Or herself?

'If you want me to,' he went on, 'I'll repeat the question. I love you, Nora. I want you to marry me. Will you?'

Then suddenly she knew. She trusted him, she loved him, but then she always had. But, even more important, what had been missing before now hit her like a thunderbolt. Beyond a doubt, what she felt were the first faint stirrings of desire.

'Yes,' she said. 'I'll marry you.' She laughed. 'I want to marry you.'

His arms came around her then and she fell against his broad chest with a sigh. This was where she belonged, where she wanted to be, safe in this strong man's arms. She raised her hands up around his neck and pressed her cheek against his, drinking in the clean, fresh scent of his hair and skin, running her fingers up into his crisp dark hair.

She felt his warm breath in her ear. 'I love you so desperately,' he murmured. 'I've tried hard not to count on anything, but lord, how I've been hoping for this!' He pulled his head back and gazed down at her, smiling crookedly. 'You're such an elusive little thing, I didn't know what to expect.' His brow furrowed. 'Do you mean it? You really will marry me?'

She nodded happily. 'And it's too late to change your mind, mister. You're hooked.'

His eyes glazed over and his hands tightened on her back. She could see the rapid rise and fall of his chest, hear his laboured breathing. For the first time, she *wanted* him to kiss her, wanted to feel his body pressed against hers. She put a hand flat on his chest over his heart to feel the heavy pounding there. Then suddenly, with no warning, she started shaking from head to foot.

He raised his head and looked down at her. 'What's the matter?' he asked with concern.

She laughed nervously. 'I'm not sure. But I think a bell just started to clang, or a drum to roll, or something like that.'

He threw back his head and laughed. 'Well, that's a good sign, isn't it?'

His head came down again and his mouth met hers in a kiss that started out gentle, tender, ten-

tative, but gradually grew more demanding. His
hands began to stroke her back, up and down, in
a steady, rhythmic motion from her shoulders to
her hips.

He murmured her name against her lips, then
raised his head to look down at her. He put a hand
on her hair, smoothing it back from her forehead,
then drew it downwards over her cheek to her neck
where it rested at the base of her throat. Then, after
a few moments, his glittering eyes never leaving
hers, he slid the hand down to move it languorously, lingeringly back and forth across her breasts.

A sharp thrill coursed through her at that first
intimate touch. She drew in a sharp breath, closed
her eyes, and let her head fall back, giving herself
up to the rising passion within her. She felt his
fingers fumbling with the buttons of her blouse,
then one hand slipped inside the opening, under
the lacy bra, to the bare flesh beneath it.

His hand began to make slow circles on her
breast, warm and sensuously rough on the tender
skin, until she felt as though she were about to burst
into flame. Then, with a hoarse sound deep in his
throat, his mouth came down on hers again with
such force that it took her breath away. It was as
though all the passion he had bottled up for the
past several months had suddenly been unleashed.
With one hand still on her breast, the other was
now clutching at her hips, his hard lower body
grinding against hers.

Nora was responding to him with a mindless sur-
render, a deep and absolute trust that she had never
before experienced with a man. There was no guile
in Mark, no question of master and mistress, no

game-playing, no vying for the upper hand. He loved her, he desired her, and she was ready to give herself to him completely.

Then, suddenly, she felt Mark's mouth leave hers, and his hand slide out from under her blouse. She opened her eyes and stared at him. He had moved back a step from her, his face turned away, his eyes cast downwards, breathing hard and obviously struggling for control.

'Mark?' she said hesitantly. 'Is something wrong?'

Finally, after another second or two, he raised his head and looked at her, a rueful smile on his flushed face. He reached out and with shaky fingers started buttoning up her blouse again. Then he put his hands on her shoulders and inhaled a lungful of air.

'I'm sorry, darling. I didn't mean to come on quite so strong. It's just that I was so happy——' He broke off and lifted his broad shoulders in an apologetic shrug. 'Well, I lost my head.'

She raised a hand and put it on his face. 'Mark, it's all right. Do you think I don't know you well enough to realise that I could have stopped you if I wanted to?'

He gave her a disbelieving look. 'I thought you weren't interested in that kind of thing with me.'

'Well, obviously I've changed my mind,' she retorted drily. 'Do you honestly think I would have agreed to marry you if I didn't love you? In every way possible?'

He shook his head. 'I'm stunned,' he said helplessly. 'I just assumed—I mean, I hoped that in time you'd come to feel the way I did, but...' Then he set his jaw firmly. 'Well, of course I'm pleased, but I still think it's best to stop right now.'

'But, Mark,' she protested. 'I'm not made of glass, you know. I just told you——'

He put a finger lightly on her lips. 'Listen, since this is the only time I'll ever be married, I want to do it right. We'll be very proper, church wedding and all. Besides, the family will be coming back for me soon. We bring Mother home today, you know.' He grinned. 'A double cause for celebration. Now, let's have that breakfast you promised me and make some plans.' He took her by the arm and led her out on to the landing. 'The first thing we have to do is set a date.'

Just then a car came down the drive, and Mark raised his head, listening. 'That must be Dad and Anna now,' he said. 'Let's go down and tell them the news.'

She put a restraining hand on his arm. 'Oh, please, not just yet, Mark. There are so many things we still have to decide.'

He opened his mouth to protest, but then immediately clamped it shut and nodded. 'All right. We'll do it your way for now. But I don't want to wait.' He took her by the hand and led her out into the hall. 'Now that I've got you, I don't want to take the chance of letting you get away.'

As they went downstairs, there came the sound of tyres squealing to a stop out in front of the house, a car door slamming, footsteps running up on to the porch.

Nora turned to Mark. 'That doesn't sound much like Anna or your father.'

Just then the door burst open and Tony flew inside.

CHAPTER EIGHT

TONY came bounding up the stairs towards them two at a time until he reached the step directly below them, panting and out of breath.

'How is she?' he demanded.

Mark put a reassuring hand on his brother's arm. 'She's OK, Tony. In fact, I'm just waiting for Anna and Dad to come back from the hospital. We're bringing her home later today.'

Tony's shoulders sagged and he sank down on the stairs. 'Thank heaven,' he breathed. 'I've been out of my mind with worry.'

Nora could only stare. This was a side of Tony she hadn't known existed. His face was grey and drawn, his fair hair hanging lankly over his forehead. He was like a frightened child, while Mark, who surely bore the brunt of running the farm and caring for his parents, was like a rock. And even though Tony's distress might have shown how much he cared for his mother, what good was caring when he fell apart at the first sign of trouble?

Just then Anna and her father drove up. When they came inside they had good news. By a stroke of luck, Mrs Leighton's doctor had made his routine visit earlier than usual that morning and pronounced her well enough to come home right then, so that they were able to bring her with them instead of having to go back later.

Mark went out to the car to get her, and as he carried her in her eyes lit on Tony first. She called his name and held her arms out to him. Watching them, Nora felt a little out of place in the family reunion, and stood at the bottom of the stairs watching them as they all went up to the invalid's bedroom.

She went into the kitchen. She'd promised to cook Mark's breakfast, and possibly the others were hungry, too. She put on a fresh pot of coffee and got out the bacon, eggs, bread and butter. There was already plenty of orange juice.

In just a few minutes, Mark walked in and came over to her side. 'You look very domestic,' he said, putting an arm around her waist. 'I like that.'

She smiled up at him. 'Well, I did promise you breakfast.' She laid strips of bacon in the pan. 'Is your mother getting all settled?'

He nodded and poured himself a glass of juice. 'Anna's taking care of it.'

'Do you think I should cook something for the others?'

'I wouldn't bother at the moment. Dad's fussing around Mother, and Tony's gone to clean up and change his clothes. He's been driving all night.'

'Then I guess he's recovered himself,' she commented drily.

'You mean the panic over my mother?' He shrugged. 'Tony's always been her favourite. You know, the bad boy who could do no wrong in her eyes.' He shook his head and smiled. 'You've got to hand it to him. He does have a knack with women.' Then he put a hand on her cheek. 'But not with you, I hope.'

She covered his hand with hers. 'No, Mark. Not with me.'

He sat down at the table then, and when the eggs and bacon were done Nora set his plate before him, poured out two cups of coffee and sat down across from him while he ate.

'We should be making some plans,' he said between bites. 'The way I figure it, we might as well get married right away. I see no reason to wait. Do you?'

She laughed. 'Only that I have an apartment full of furniture and all my personal belongings still back in Washington, not to mention a bank account, such as it is, and a lease that still has six months to run.'

He waved his fork in the air. 'Those are minor matters. We can go clear out your apartment later, and deal with all those other things at the same time.'

She leaned her elbow on the table and rested her chin in her hand. 'You make it all sound so simple.'

He finished the last bite of food, leaned back in his chair and gazed fondly at her. 'It is. I'm a simple man, remember? The important thing is getting married as soon as possible.' He leaned forward and reached across the table to put his hand on her arm. 'I don't want to wait.'

She shook her head. 'No. I don't either.'

'Why not make it next weekend, then? Say, Saturday. We can get a licence during the week, and I'm sure Anna and Mother between them will be overjoyed at the prospect of arranging for the church and all the trimmings.'

'Hey, Mark, hold on. Not so fast. I have a job, remember? I told them I'd be back on Monday.'

He gave her a stricken look. 'Lord, I didn't even think of that. I'm sorry. I was just taking it for granted you'd want to live here, but if your job means a lot to you...' His voice trailed off.

Nora thought about her job for perhaps the second time since she'd left Washington to come to the farm—the position as director she hadn't got, the daily drudgery that led nowhere, the loneliness of her solitary apartment, the hideous daily commute. And she knew.

'No,' she stated firmly. 'That job has no future. I won't mind giving it up in the least. In fact, it will be a pleasure.'

The relief on his face was so heartfelt it was almost funny. 'If you want to work, there's plenty to do here, especially for someone good at figures. We'll work something out.' His dark eyes were full of concern. 'I want you to be happy, Nora.'

'You make me happy, Mark,' she said softly. 'I'll call the office on Monday and tell them I won't be coming back. But,' she went on in a brisker tone, 'there is the matter of my parents. We're not all that close, but knowing my mother she'd never speak to me again if I got married without her being there.'

'Well, let's get them here.'

She frowned. 'That's just the problem. I don't know where they are, except that it's probably somewhere back in the States by now.' She brightened. 'I gave her your number before we left. She'll probably be calling me any day.'

'I'll hire detectives to find them if I have to,' he said. 'In the meantime, can we plan on next Saturday for the wedding?'

'All right, Mark. If that's what you want.'

Just then Tony came in, his old jaunty step back, whistling under his breath. Nora and Mark both looked up at him when he appeared in the doorway, and he stopped short, his eyes travelling from one to the other.

'Aha,' he said slowly. 'Caught in the act. What's going on?'

Mark gave Nora an enquiring look, and when she nodded he stood up and walked over to his brother. 'Nora and I are going to be married,' he said.

Tony's mouth fell open. 'I don't believe it,' he said on a long-drawn-out breath.

'Well, you'd better, brother,' Mark said, 'because it's true.'

Recovering from his surprise, Tony reached over and slapped Mark heartily on the back. 'Well, good for you, old boy. I didn't know you had it in you.'

Once again Nora bridled at the condescending tone, but firmly resolved to keep quiet about it. It would be a mistake to interfere. Mark didn't need her to defend him.

'How about some breakfast, Tony?' she asked instead. 'If you've been travelling all night you must be hungry.'

'That sounds great.' He sat down at the table. 'I could use a glass of that orange juice first.'

Nora silently poured out a glass of juice and took it over to the table, biting back a sharp comment at his bland assumption she was there to wait on him. All that little-boy charm masked was a spoiled rotten child!

'Guess I'll go up and see if Mother needs anything,' Mark said, moving towards the door. 'Then I might as well change into my work clothes and get some of the chores done down at the stables.'

When he was gone there was dead silence in the room for a while, broken only by the sizzling of the bacon in the pan.

Finally, Tony spoke. 'That coffee smells good.'

'It is,' she said curtly. 'Why don't you get up and pour yourself a cup?'

If he was surprised at her tone, he didn't let on. And he did get up and pour his own coffee. When his breakfast was finished she handed it to him, then started to clear away Mark's dishes.

'So,' Tony said. 'When's the wedding to be?'

'Soon. We're thinking about next Saturday, depending on whether I can get hold of my parents.'

After a few more feeble efforts at conversation that elicited the same terse replies, Tony kept quiet and ate his breakfast while Nora ran hot water into the sink to do the dishes. When he was through, he got up and came to stand at her side. She ignored him, until finally he cleared his throat.

'Uh—Nora,' he said.

'Yes. What is it?'

'About what happened last time I was home— you know, my coming on to you the way I did, I want to apologise for that. I was out of line. It'll never happen again, I promise.'

She turned to him and smiled, softening in spite of herself at the apparently sincere apology. After all, if he was going to be her brother-in-law, they'd have to make peace eventually.

'All right, Tony,' she said. 'Apology accepted. Let's just forget it ever happened.'

He put an arm around her shoulders and leaned down to kiss her on the cheek. She was so surprised by the unexpected gesture that she instinctively pulled her head back and glared at him. But the look in his eyes was so unthreatening that she took the token of affection as it apparently was intended—a brotherly peck.

Then, from behind them, came Mark's voice. 'Well, what's going on here? Trying to steal my girl, Tony?'

His tone was light, but Nora immediately sensed an undercurrent of genuine hostility in it. She turned around to face him. He was coming towards them in long, purposeful strides, smiling with his mouth, but not his eyes.

Tony raised his hands in mock innocence. 'Who, me? Never! I was just welcoming Nora into the family.' He started towards the door. 'Now I guess I'll go up and see Mother.'

Mark stood aside as Tony breezed past him and stood there looking after him even after he was long gone out of sight. Then he turned to Nora.

'For some reason, I don't quite trust that brother of mine around you,' he said lightly, trying to make a joke of it.

But Nora could tell he was genuinely upset. She put her arms around his waist and rested her cheek against his chest, hugging him tightly. He seemed stiff and withdrawn in her arms, and she looked up at him.

'I love you, Mark,' she murmured. 'It's you I want to marry.'

His tense features relaxed slightly, but the dark eyes were still troubled. 'I don't know,' he said slowly. 'Coming in here, seeing you together like that, I suddenly couldn't help noticing how strongly Tony resembled that guy in the picture I saw that night in your bedroom.'

Nora dropped her eyes from his and bit her lip, thinking fast. How much should she tell him? She'd learned from experience that the best way to deal with Mark was to be absolutely honest with him. She gazed up at him again.

'All right, Mark,' she said at last. 'There is a resemblance. I noticed it, too, the first time I saw Tony. And I admit that somehow I used to have the crazy idea that only a certain kind of man appealed to me. Men like Stephen. And, I guess, like Tony.'

She searched his face, but his expression was sober, and he only seemed to be listening intently to her. She waved a hand in the air. 'And not just their physical appearance, although I thought that was part of it. I already told you how I was always drawn to problem men, intense, self-absorbed types.' She tightened her hold on him. 'You've changed all that for me. Now I know what it's like to be loved by a real man.'

He smiled at last. 'Well, I don't know about that, but I do know I can promise you absolute loyalty and enduring love.' He stopped short, his face sober again, even solemn, and put a hand on her cheek. 'You should understand, Nora, that I'm a man of absolute commitment. It's taken me thirty-eight years to find the one woman I could devote my life to.' His hand moved up into her hair. 'I'll be a good husband to you,' he went on. 'But I will never share you.' Then his gaze softened. 'Does that sound terribly macho and possessive?'

She couldn't help but think of his outburst of temper on the day they'd arrived at the farm, his reaction to her explanation of why she'd had Stephen's picture in her bedroom. He *was* a possessive man, even a jealous one, and he did have a temper. But wasn't that all part of his appeal?

'No,' she replied at last. 'It sounds wonderful.'

By now there wasn't a doubt left in her mind that she did love Mark and want to marry him, but that last display of jealousy still nagged occasionally at the back of her mind during those next few happy days. She tried to pass the whole episode off as trivial, but it wouldn't quite go away and continued to loom larger and larger.

She had to face the fact that, beneath his self-contained exterior, Mark was an intensely jealous man. When she'd told him about Stephen's last visit, he had seemed actually murderous. While his possessiveness revealed depths of emotion that she found highly flattering in one way, it almost frightened her in another. She wished he hadn't broken off his lovemaking so abruptly that day in his room. Maybe if she belonged to him completely, his suspicions would be cured. She'd told him then she wasn't made of glass, but he had been firm in his belief that they should wait.

At the time, she'd thought it merely amusing, another indication of his high-minded moral code, which was one of the things she'd come to love about him most. But that, coupled with the jealousy, made her worry that he was putting her on a pedestal she couldn't possibly hope to sustain.

Not that she had any reservations about her ability to remain faithful to him, to the death. In her previous fatal obsessions with the wrong kind of man she had been searching for someone she could give her trust and loyalty to forever. Now she'd found him. But his jealous temper was something they'd definitely have to settle.

From then on everything began to fall into place, just as though the gods were really on their side, smiling at them. When they told Mark's family their news, they were as pleased as he had predicted they'd be, and Anna happily made plans to take charge of all the arrangements, with her mother as chief adviser.

On Sunday afternoon Nora's mother did call her at last from their new condo in the Georgetown district of Washington.

'How have you been?' her mother asked when she'd finally finished telling Nora all about it.

'All right,' Nora replied. 'Well, actually,' she went on with a little laugh, 'more than all right. Brace yourself, Mother. I'm getting married. His name is Mark Leighton.'

'Oh, how wonderful! I'm so pleased.' She paused a moment. 'Nora, isn't that the name of the people you're staying with?'

'As a matter of fact it is.'

'Well, aren't you the sly one! Have you set a date? I hope you're not going to elope. I don't want to miss my only daughter's wedding.'

'We're thinking about this coming Saturday, here in the church near Mark's farm. His mother and sister are making all the arrangements. Can you make it then?'

'Of course. I may have a problem with your father, he's so tired of travelling, but I think in the end I can convince him to make the trip.'

The time did pass, and it was Friday at last. Tomorrow was her wedding day. The church was reserved for eleven o'clock, the flowers ordered, and they planned to spend their honeymoon in Bermuda, with a stop along the way in Washington to take care of Nora's unfinished business. She'd decided in the end to give her notice at work in person first thing Monday morning.

Her parents arrived late that morning. It was a beautiful day, a harbinger, Nora hoped, of her future life as Mark Leighton's wife. Although the air was still biting cold and the landscape bleak, the sun was shining overhead, and here and there in the garden the first early crocuses were showing traces of colour.

Nora had been apprehensive all that morning as to how the two families would get along. They were so different. During the flurry of introductions, Mark caught her eye and gave her a reassuring grin, as though he sensed her nervousness. Then he winked at her and skirted around the others to stand by her side.

As they all drifted into the house, a polite but rather heated discussion had already begun about her parents' accommodation. Her mother was insisting on staying at the motel in the nearby town, and Anna was protesting.

'But we planned to have you stay here with us,' she said.

As they all stood there in the entry hall, Nora glanced at her mother. She had that look about her, the one that would brook no opposition. The stiff smile, the rigid posture, the fists clenched at her sides, spoke volumes about her state of mind.

For his part, her father was eyeing Anna in a heavy-lidded gaze of appraisal, as though calculating his chances, and it was also obvious to Nora just why her mother was being so stubborn. It was clearly time for her to take a firm hand.

'Anna,' she said, going up to her. 'It's no use arguing with my mother once she has her mind made up.' She laughed to take the sting out of her words and turned to her mother. 'Right, Mother?'

The older woman relaxed visibly. 'It's very kind of you to offer to let us stay here,' she said in a calmer tone. 'But we really would feel better staying on our own.' She turned to her husband. 'Right, William?'

'Whatever you say,' he replied with a shrug. 'It makes no difference to me.'

Apparently Anna knew when to give up. 'Well, at least come back and have dinner with us tonight,' she said with a sigh. 'We were counting on that.'

Since it had been months since Nora had even seen her parents, she decided to drive into town with them so they could have a private family visit, their last before her wedding. It was only a short distance of about ten miles, and on the way Nora was painfully aware of the almost palpable tension between her parents.

Her father was scowling in concentration at the wheel, driving too fast as always, her mother sitting rigidly by his side wrapped in stony silence and smoking steadily. Nora wondered if she had caught him in a new escapade—already! They'd only been back in the States for a few weeks.

After they got settled in their motel, they went to a nearby café for lunch. Although she was genuinely fond of both her mother and father, she viewed them now from an entirely new perspective. In the months they had been gone, her life had changed dramatically. Having met Mark and fallen in love with him, she was simply not the person she had been the last time she'd seen them.

She'd always especially adored her father, even though there was no denying his feckless behaviour. In fact, unconsciously she'd blamed her mother— her extravagance, her preoccupation with her social contacts, her appearance—as responsible for his wandering eye, even, Nora suspected, his outright infidelities.

Watching them now as they ate, her mother in her latest Paris creation and still very beautiful even in middle age, her father with his typical expression of intense self-absorption, she began to wonder if perhaps all along it hadn't actually been her mother who was the strong one.

Then, all of a sudden, it hit her. Could it be that her father, with his slim build and fair good looks, was the model for her past rotten taste in men? Viewing him now from a colder, more detached point of view, she saw clearly that he could be an older version of Stephen Kincaid or Tony Leighton, or any one of a long series of unsuitable men.

It was an interesting speculation, and quite an eye-opener. But although it explained a lot about the mistakes she'd made in the past, it would take an army of psychiatrists to figure it out, and there was no point dwelling on it now. Whatever the cause, she was cured at last, and she could hardly blame her father for being the man he was.

They spent the entire meal talking about their trip, the yachts they had been invited on, the parties they'd attended, the fine homes they'd stayed in. Finally, when they'd finished eating, her mother lit a long, thin cigarette, leaned back languorously in her chair, and gazed at Nora through the clouds of smoke billowing around her.

'Now, darling,' she said. 'I want to hear all about this man you're going to marry. He seems very nice. Rather quiet, not a lot of personality like his brother, but nice.'

'He must be rich,' her father put in. 'When I was with the Department of the Interior we had many dealings with these horse-breeders in the Shenandoah Valley. They're all loaded.'

Nora smiled. Their reactions were so typical and, she realised for the first time, so shallow. If that was where she'd learned her values, it was no wonder she'd spent half her life falling in love with the wrong kind of man. She thought about Mark, so steady, so forthright and unassuming, so *real*!

'Well,' she finally replied, 'I don't know about rich. It belongs to the whole family, not just Mark.'

'Have you chosen your wedding dress yet?' her mother asked.

Nora stared at her. 'Why, no,' she said slowly. 'Everything has happened so fast, I haven't even thought about it.'

Her mother gave her an exasperated look. 'That's so like you, Nora.' She nodded sharply and ground out her cigarette in the large crystal ashtray. 'Well, we'd better take care of that right away. We should be able to find something suitable, even here in the back of beyond.'

'Oh, Mother, I don't think——'

'And we really should do something about your hair,' her mother went on inexorably. She reached over and ran a hand over Nora's sleek dark cap. 'It's pretty enough that way for a working girl, but now that you're going to be the lady of the manor, so to speak, you should make more of an effort.'

Nora only laughed. She had no intention of allowing her mother to transform her into a carbon copy of herself. Clearly she was going to have a battle of wills on her hands. She wouldn't argue the point, but she was determined to win that battle.

That night after dinner, when they were all gathered at the farm in the spacious living-room before a roaring fire, Nora sat silently watching the others as they interacted, and especially comparing Mark and Tony. How could brothers be so different?

Tony, with his easy charm, had obviously entranced her mother. He and his own mother were on either side of her on the couch, showing her an album of family photographs, and at each page he made an amusing remark, sending both women into gales of appreciative laughter. For his part, Mark sat quietly in a nearby chair, enjoying their fun, but making no attempt to compete with the ebullient Tony.

The party broke up early, not quite ten o'clock, and soon after Nora's parents left to go back to their motel the Leighton family, all early risers, went up to bed, leaving Nora and Mark alone in the living-room.

The fire was burning low by then, and when the others were gone he turned to her. She was sitting under the lamp in a comfortable easy-chair, finally able to relax. She put her head back, closed her eyes and sighed contentedly.

'What's the sigh for?' he asked, coming over to her.

She looked up at him with a smile. 'It's been quite a day.'

He nodded. 'Would you like a drink?'

'No, thanks. That would put me right to sleep.'

'I could build up the fire,' he said. 'Unless you're too tired and want to turn in.'

'No. It's pleasant just to sit here in the quiet.'

He sat down on the arm of her chair and leaned over her. 'I enjoyed meeting your parents,' he said in a low voice. 'But it's good to have some time alone.' He put a hand on her face. 'I've been waiting for a chance to touch you all day.'

She raised her face to his and smiled up at him. 'Well, the waiting is almost over now.'

He slipped his other arm around her and bent his head down lower. As his lips met hers in a kiss of ineffable sweetness, a wave of tenderness and love swept over her. A vision of her future as Mark's wife rose up before her like the fulfilment of all her deepest desires. Nothing could ever possibly go wrong again with this man's love to lean on.

Gradually the pressure of his mouth increased on hers. The hand on her cheek slid down to grasp the base of her throat, then lower to rest tenderly on her breast. He raised his head and looked down at her. In the glow of the dim lamplight his dark eyes glittered, and his quickening breath was warm on her face.

'Lord, I want you so badly, darling,' he said huskily.

'I know,' she whispered. 'I want you, too, Mark.'

Just then a voice came from the direction of the stairs, calling his name softly. He jerked his head up, frowning at the interruption, rose to his feet and walked slowly towards the front hallway.

'Yes?' he called. 'What is it?'

Then Nora heard Anna's low voice. 'I'm sorry, Mark, but Mother insisted I remind you to lock up before you go to bed. You know how she worries.'

The short exchange only took a few seconds, but by then the spell was broken. Worn out anyway from the gruelling day, Nora had risen to her feet by the time he came back to her, a rueful half-smile creasing his face.

He put his hands on her shoulders and laughed shortly. 'I guess this is neither the time nor the place for what I have in mind,' he said.

'Never mind. Tomorrow it'll all be over.'

He gathered her into his arms and held her close, his face buried in her hair. 'I can hardly believe it. It seems too good to be true.' Then with a sigh he released her, his hands hanging at his sides. 'Come on, I'd better walk you to your room—and leave you there for the last time, for the rest of our lives.'

That night in bed, Nora was far too excited about her wedding to sleep. She would doze off, only to wake up shortly to find it was still dark. Mark's parting words kept echoing in her mind. This would be the last night she would sleep alone. Tomorrow she would be married to Mark Leighton.

She wondered if all brides were this jumpy on the eve before their weddings. Finally, she turned on the light and glanced at the bedside clock. It was two o'clock in the morning, and she hadn't slept more than a few hours. Maybe some warm milk would do the trick. She slipped out of bed, put on her robe and slippers and padded down the hall towards the kitchen.

As she approached, she could see that a light was burning. Hoping it might be Mark, she quickened her step, already smiling at the prospect of one more goodnight kiss. But when she got inside, it wasn't Mark. Sitting at the kitchen table, wearing only the bottoms to a blue pair of pyjamas and sipping what looked like a very potent drink, was Tony. A bottle of bourbon was on the table before him.

It was too late to turn and run. He'd already seen her and was staring directly at her. Besides, what was the point? They would be brother and sister by tomorrow, even living in the same house. He had apologised sincerely for that one ugly episode and they had made their peace. She had nothing to fear from him—or herself. She did wish he had more clothes on, but she might as well get used to that, too.

She smiled and walked inside. 'I see you can't sleep, either,' she said. She went past him and walked over to the fridge. 'I thought I'd heat myself a glass of milk.'

Tony held up his glass. 'This is more effective.'

'What is it?'

'Bourbon.'

She laughed. 'You might be right.'

She reached in the cupboard and took out a glass, then sat down next to him while he poured out a measure of bourbon. He handed it to her, then raised his glass in a toast.

'Here's to you and Mark,' he said. 'May you live long and prosper.' He took a healthy swallow of his drink. 'As I have no doubt you will.'

The first sip of the bourbon stung Nora's throat, but as it went down it warmed her, and she could feel her tense muscles relaxing. She took another sip and looked at Tony, who was strangely silent. His face was drawn, his eyes glazed over dully and staring down at the glass in his hand, an intense, brooding expression on his face. Nora wondered if he might be ill.

'You don't look too sharp, Tony,' she said hesitantly. 'I hope our best man isn't going to get sick on us.'

'No,' he said quietly. 'It's not that.' He turned to her. 'I was just lying in bed thinking about you and Mark, how I envied you, what you two have that I probably never will.'

She stared at him, shocked by this admission from such a self-assured man. 'Why, Tony, that's not true. You just haven't found the right person yet.' She reached out and put a hand on his arm. 'Besides, you're only a boy.'

He had to smile at that. 'Sure, a thirty-two-year-old boy. And one of these days I'll be a forty-year-old boy. Then fifty.' He shook his head sadly. 'I don't know, Nora. I've been with a lot of women in my time, and you can take my word for it, there aren't many around like you.'

'Maybe that's because there aren't many men around like Mark,' she said softly. 'You could learn a lot from him, you know.'

He gave her a sharp look. 'You might be right.' He rose abruptly to his feet, yawned and stretched. 'Well, I guess I'll try again to get some sleep.' He picked up the bottle of bourbon and carried it over to the counter, then turned back to her and held it up in the air. 'Do you want any more of this?'

'No, thanks. I can't even finish what you gave me.' She got up from her chair and went to his side. 'Here,' she said, holding out a hand. 'Give me your glass and I'll rinse them both out. We don't want the family to come down in the morning and think we had a late-night drinking orgy.'

He stood leaning back against the counter, his arms folded across his chest, watching her while she rinsed out the glasses and set them on the draining-board to dry. When she'd finished, she wiped her hands on a towel and turned to him with a smile.

'Well, goodnight, Tony. Let's hope your remedy works and we can both get some sleep now.'

He laughed. 'It always has in the past.' He gazed at her fondly. 'And thanks for the pep talk, Nora.'

She looked up at him and touched his cheek lightly. 'Don't worry, Tony. Some day Miss Right will come along for you.'

When he put an arm around her shoulder and bent down to kiss her on the cheek, it seemed like the most natural thing in the world, a simple token of brotherly affection. The liquor had warmed her, relieved her tension, and she was so full of her own happiness that she was suffused with a warm glow towards all humanity.

Just then, from the shadows beyond the doorway, came Mark's voice, low, intense, and throbbing with emotion. 'Well, isn't this a cosy little scene?'

Before Nora could utter a word, he strode purposefully into the room and made straight for Tony. He grabbed him by the scruff of the neck, pulled him away from Nora, and in one sweeping blow of his powerful fist knocked him to the floor.

CHAPTER NINE

BY THE time Mark was finished with him, Tony lay bruised and bleeding at his feet. Nora felt she should go to him, to try to help him in case he was seriously hurt, but she couldn't move. She could only stand there horrified, one hand at her throat, the other over her mouth. Although it never entered her head that Mark would harm her, the violence of his attack on Tony had really frightened her.

He was standing there glaring down at his brother, his hands still bunched into fists, his chest heaving, his mouth set in a grim line, his face thunderous.

Finally, Tony groaned and stumbled to his feet. A thin trickle of blood ran down his chin from a cut on his lip, but other than that he seemed to be unharmed. Dazedly, he looked around, shook his head, then ran a hand through his hair and focused his bloodshot eyes on Mark.

'OK, brother,' he mumbled. 'I guess I had that coming.'

'You're damn right you had it coming,' Mark growled in a low, menacing tone. 'And for a hell of a long time. You've always taken everything I've ever wanted, haven't you, Tony? Always worked it so that you got the best horse, the best education, and now you had to have my girl, too.' He gestured toward Nora, who was cowering in a corner, paralysed. 'All right,' he snarled. 'You can have her.'

'Listen, Mark,' Tony began haltingly. 'It wasn't like that——'

'Get out, Tony,' Mark broke in contemptuously.

Tony closed his mouth. He looked at Nora and shrugged apologetically. Then he turned and walked slowly over to the door.

When he was gone, Mark stood there for a moment without speaking. Except for the ticking of the clock on the wall, the room was utterly silent. Then, slowly, he turned and looked at her.

She searched his face, trying to read his thoughts, but the impassive expression there told her nothing. Then something flickered momentarily in the depths of his dark eyes, and he took a step towards her.

She raised a hand to him. 'Mark, it's not what you think,' she began.

He was directly before her now, looking down at her. She gazed up at him, still searching for some clue to his feelings about her. All the anger seemed to have drained out of him, and now what she saw in his eyes was a terrible pain.

'You wanted excitement, was that it, Nora?' he asked in a low, expressionless monotone. 'I was too dull for you.'

'No!' she cried. 'It wasn't like that. You've got the wrong idea entirely. Maybe you're right—maybe Tony did deserve it. I'll admit that the last time he was home he made a stupid pass at me. But we had it out then, and he never tried it again. This time it was entirely different.'

'You were kissing him, and not for the first time. He wasn't forcing you.'

She took a deep breath. How could she explain so that he would understand? She had to think, try to make her voice calm, to defuse the tense situation.

'All right, Mark,' she said at last. 'For one second I let him kiss me. One second! And that's what you saw.'

'One second is enough!' he barked.

'But it was only as a brother to a sister, Mark, I swear it.'

'Brother to sister?' He gestured towards the bottle of bourbon, which was still sitting on the counter. 'You were drinking together, all alone in here, half dressed!' He narrowed his eyes into slits. 'I told you once I'd never share you. I knew you didn't love me the way I loved you. That was all right. I thought I could make you happy, take care of you. But it wasn't enough, was it?'

'Mark, I *do* love you!' she wailed. 'You know I do. You're what I want, all I want.'

He shook his head. 'I won't share you,' he repeated. Then he bared his teeth in a parody of a smile. 'But if it's excitement you want, I'll give it to you—something to remember me by.'

He took a step towards her. She shrank back, clutching the openings of her robe together and staring at him, her eyes wide with sudden apprehension. He reached out and grasped both her hands in one of his, and forced her arms up over her head. The robe fell open, revealing the silky pink nightgown she wore beneath it.

Then, in one swift movement, his other hand shot out. Strong fingers took hold of the low neckline of her gown and ripped the flimsy material down the centre. Still holding her hands over her head, he crushed his hard body against hers, grinding against her and forcing her back against the counter until she was almost bent over backwards. His open mouth came down on hers, his tongue forcing entry, hot and demanding.

She felt his large hand now at her breasts, kneading and clutching at them with urgent, punishing strokes. He tore his mouth away, raised his head and glared down at her, breathing hard, his normally calm brown eyes ablaze with a powerful emotion he could barely control.

She cowered back from him, hardly daring to breathe, stifling back a cry, waiting for the next onslaught. But, instead, his shoulders slumped defeatedly and he took a backward step. He gave her one last look, a strange look mingled of anger and unutterable sorrow. Then he turned abruptly and stalked away from her.

When he was gone, she stood there, trembling, clutching her torn nightgown together, too dazed to move. After several long moments, she managed to retie her robe. Then she walked slowly out of the kitchen, switching off the light as she went. She stumbled blindly in the dark out to the telephone in the front hall.

The one thought on her mind was to get out of there, away from that house, away from Mark. The anger she'd seen in him once before when she'd told him about Stephen's last visit was only a mild upset compared to the insane jealousy he'd displayed tonight. There was no way she could ever live with that. It didn't matter. Clearly he didn't want her any more.

By the dim light that shone inside from the front porch she could just manage to look up the number of the motel where her parents were staying. With shaky fingers, and praying Mark hadn't woken the whole house, she dialled the number. When the sleepy clerk answered, she asked for her parents' room.

After ten rings her mother finally answered.

'Mother, this is Nora,' she said in a low, hushed voice. 'You've got to get Daddy up and come out here to the farm and get me right away.'

'What in the world——?'

'Please, Mother, don't ask me any questions. I'll explain everything later. Just do this for me, I beg you. I have to get out of this house tonight, and I have nowhere else to turn.'

When her bewildered mother finally agreed to do as she asked, Nora went swiftly down to her room. She threw on some clothes and began emptying drawers, tossing her clothes and personal belongings into her suitcase any which way. As she packed, she thought of writing a note to Anna, but what could she say? Better leave the explanations up to Mark.

When she was through she let herself out of the front door into the dark, cold night and started walking down the drive to open the gate for her father.

It was past noon the next day when they arrived back in Washington. During the entire drive, by tacit agreement, the reason for Nora's hurried flight from Leightons wasn't mentioned.

When they dropped her off in front of her building, she said a hasty goodbye, thanked them again and told her mother she'd call her soon. Then she trudged wearily up the stairs to her apartment, let herself in and left her bag just inside the door while she went through the cold rooms, turning on heat and making sure nothing had been disturbed in her absence.

As she surveyed her cluttered living-room, she was appalled that she could have gone off and left it in such a mess. She wasn't the world's greatest housekeeper, but was generally neater than that. They had left Washington three weeks ago in such a hurry that Mark's couch-bed was still unmade, their breakfast dishes still on the draining-board.

It would take her the rest of the weekend to get the place in decent shape, but that was probably for the best. She needed just that kind of mindless occupation to keep from dwelling on her shattered romance, her broken dreams.

As she glanced around, the apartment suddenly seemed terribly bleak and lonely compared to the warmth and clutter of the farmhouse. Today was to have been her wedding day. Then, as the tears began to well up in her eyes, she sank slowly down on the couch Mark had slept in and let them come at last.

The following Monday morning, Nora stood in line at her bus-stop at the usual time under a leaden sky, ready for her first day back at work in three weeks. She was profoundly grateful now that she'd waited to give in her notice at work and had told no one there of her wedding plans.

The bus finally arrived, ten minutes late, and she climbed aboard in the press of other commuters. She found a seat way in the back, and, as they bumped their way down to the centre of town, she thought about those happy days at the farm. She'd been so desperate to leave at the time, yet ever since she'd arrived home she'd almost constantly wondered why.

Maybe she should have stayed and fought for what she wanted. Mark was ordinarily the mildest of men. He would have calmed down by morning. He hadn't really hurt her, and no doubt Tony had had the beating coming to him, not for what had happened that night, but for a long history of self-indulgence at his brother's expense, including the pass he'd once made at her.

But she knew she was only grasping at straws. Mark was a man of powerful and lasting emotion. He hated as strongly as he loved. If she'd stayed and tried to reason with him, it wouldn't have done any good. Her blood still ran cold every time she recalled the look on his face when he'd seen her and Tony together that night. Better to have found out before she'd married him. How could she have lived with a man whose jealous temper could explode at any time?

When she stepped off the bus and walked the half-block to her office, she hesitated at the door, stopped cold by a sudden attack of nerves. She'd taken an early bus just so she should be the first to arrive and wouldn't have to make a grand entrance. Although she was glad in a way to be getting back to work, just for something to do, she dreaded having to answer questions about the reason for her absence.

She took a deep breath, pushed the door open and went inside. It was eerily quiet, and she was glad to see that no one else was there yet. As she was taking off her coat, however, the front door opened, letting in a gust of cold air, and she turned around to see Jackie walking towards her.

'Well, as I live and breathe!' Jackie cried, stopping short and staring. 'What in the world are you doing here? I thought you were laid up with a broken ankle?'

'Not broken, just sprained. And it's all healed. How have things been around here while I was gone?'

A few other people were straggling in through the door by now, and as soon as Jackie had hung up her coat she grabbed Nora's arm and started walking towards the gate in the counter.

'Let's go to your office,' she said under her breath. 'I've got some hot news for you.'

Inside Nora's room, Jackie shut the door behind them, gave Nora a conspiratorial look, and glanced suspiciously around, as though expecting to uncover spies lurking in the corners.

'Jackie!' Nora said with a laugh. 'What's going on?'

'You won't believe this,' Jackie said in a hushed *sotto voce*. 'You know the new director?'

Nora nodded. 'Mrs Smith.'

'Right. Well, she spent one day here then didn't show up again for a week. We heard later that Personnel sent someone to her home to see what was wrong and they found her passed out cold in an alcoholic stupor.'

'Oh, Jackie, how awful!'

'That isn't all. In the meantime, it seems that Personnel is finally getting their act together and about to name a new director. The one who should have had the job in the first place.' She grinned broadly. 'That's right, honey. It looks as though you're going to get it after all.'

Nora sank down slowly in her chair. She could hardly believe it. She gazed blankly at Jackie, who looked as pleased as though she'd invented the job and made the decision herself. Jackie came over to the desk and braced her hands on the top, leaning over.

'I couldn't resist giving you the scoop myself, but don't let on you already know when they tell you about it.' She glanced at her watch. 'I'd better go now. How about lunch today?'

Nora shook her head slowly. 'Not today, Jackie. I've got three weeks' work to catch up on.' She wrinkled her forehead. 'Jackie, are you sure about Mrs Smith?'

Jackie nodded vehemently and held a hand up. 'Scout's honour. It's the gospel truth. You wait and see.'

She turned to leave, but before she got halfway to the door she turned around, a bemused expression on her face. 'Where in the heck have you been for the past three weeks? I tried to call you at home several times, but never got an answer. Were you in the hospital or what?'

'Oh, no, I wasn't hurt that badly. I just spent some time at a friend's farm in Virginia.'

'A friend? What friend?'

'Just a friend.'

'Hey, doesn't that Leighton guy have a farm in Virginia? You know, I thought right from the beginning that he was more than mildly interested in you.'

'Jackie, I've never known anyone who could jump to conclusions the way you do. What makes you think I'd even be invited to Mark's farm, much less go?'

There was a dramatic silence. Then Jackie said, 'Mark?'

Nora was caught and she knew it. 'All right. That's where I was. Now, are you happy? But don't make a big thing out of it. We're only friends. He just happened to be there when I got hurt, and very kindly offered to let me recuperate at his place— with his sister and parents present every minute.'

'Well, you look wonderful, I'll say that for you,' Jackie commented, eyeing her up and down. She glanced at her watch. 'Got to run now, but I'll expect all the details later.'

That very afternoon the head of Personnel called Nora to his office to tell her that the director's job was indeed hers if she wanted it. When she agreed, he arranged to have her attend an indoctrination course in another building for two weeks.

The course consisted of a series of boring lectures, and she saw right away that the job would entail a profound departure from her old one. She would no longer do any actual accounting work, but would have new responsibilities she wasn't sure she could handle.

When she actually took over her duties at the end of the course, it turned out to be more demanding than she had thought, and much more of a headache. Her main functions were to stay within the department's budget, determine policy and see that it was carried out, and she soon found there was an enormous difference between working with figures and handling people.

It didn't take her long to realise that, in spite of the added pay and heightened prestige, it wouldn't be very congenial work. Figures were her strong point, not people, and, although it was true that her old job wasn't going anywhere, she had at least felt competent to perform it.

Still, there was one enormous advantage to her increased responsibility, even outside of the fact that it was an upward step in the bureaucratic hierarchy, and that was that it kept her mind so occupied she couldn't think about Mark, at least during working hours. She'd been back in Washington for almost a month now and hadn't heard a word from him. Nor had she really expected to.

There were moments in that time, especially during the long, lonely evenings, that she was tempted to call him or write to him, to try once again to explain what had happened that night with Tony. In fact twice she had actually gone to the telephone and started to dial his number.

But her feelings about him were still so confused that in the end she always decided not to. In the deep dark recesses of her heart she still loved him and missed him terribly, his strong, steady presence, his devotion to her, his dependability, the passion he had finally evoked in her. But she had no idea what she could possibly do about it, or even if she should.

Part of her new job was to referee disputes, not only among the staff but with certain unhappy clients. It seemed as though she spent her entire working life either looking for ways to save money or soothing wounded egos.

She'd been at the job for over six weeks when Jackie burst into her office one morning looking even more harried and wild-eyed than usual. Nora glanced up from her work and sighed inwardly, afraid of what was coming. Her volatile friend was engaged in a running dispute with the young man who had taken over Nora's old job, and each day seemed to bring a new complaint.

'Yes, Jackie,' she said. 'Another problem with Derek?'

'Not this time,' Jackie said breathlessly. 'I've got a guy out there who's so upset he's threatening to go to his congressman. I've spent the last hour with him trying to explain things, but he's the most stubborn case I've ever come across. Now he's insisting on speaking to the director and——'

'OK, Jackie, send him in. And you'd better bring in the file.'

Jackie nodded and gave her a little salute on her way out of the door. 'Thanks, boss,' she said with a grin.

When she was gone, Nora got up from her chair and went over to the coat rack beside the window to retrieve her suit jacket. As she slipped into it, she glanced outside. It was March, almost spring, the last cruel winds of winter over, the cherry trees along The Mall just leafing out into a pale green haze, and it occurred to her how lovely the farm must be at this time of year.

In a few moments she heard her door open and close, and she turned around, all primed to deal with Jackie's problem. When she saw Mark standing there just inside the door, the shock was so great that a sudden wave of dizziness passed over her. She blinked, swaying slightly, and grasped the sill of the window for support.

'Hello, Nora,' he said quietly.

Somehow the familiar sound of his calm voice steadied her. She straightened her shoulders, raised her chin and walked over to stand behind her desk.

'Hello, Mark,' she said. 'What can I do for you?'

'Well, I don't actually have a tax problem this time.' He tried a smile, but it didn't quite work, and his face darkened. 'I guess I should apologise for tricking you into seeing me, but I figured it was probably the only way I'd get in.'

'You haven't tried any other way, have you?' she snapped, annoyed. 'You haven't called, haven't written, haven't come to see me, not once, in over two months.'

'Would it have done me any good if I had?' he asked bleakly. 'Would you have talked to me?'

She looked down at her hands, which were twisted together tightly on top of the desk. 'I don't know,' she said in a low voice.

'Will you talk to me now? Or, rather, let me talk?'

She sighed wearily and raised her head. 'Yes, if it'll make you feel any better. But there really isn't much point. I think you said all you needed to that last night at the farm. You accused me of something pretty nasty, Mark, when you thought Tony and I...'

He held up a hand and took one step closer. 'I know,' he muttered. 'I was an idiot. I think I knew it even then. Not so much for the beating I gave

Tony—he's had that coming for years. I only wish I'd done it when he was ten years old instead of waiting until you were involved.' He put his hand on the back of the chair. 'Can I sit down?'

She nodded and slid gratefully down into her own chair. She folded her arms in front of her and waited for him to go on.

'I guess I should explain about me and Tony,' he began. 'First of all, it never really bothered me that he was mother's favourite. Dad and I were always close. Anna, too. The three of us are rather solitary people, and the way my mother doted on Tony was always kind of a family joke. No one ever took it seriously before.' He shrugged. 'I don't know, maybe I resented it during the years we were growing up more than I ever let on.'

He took a deep breath. 'At any rate,' he went on, 'what I'm trying to say is that I'm not worried about Tony. He can take care of himself. What I can't forgive myself for is what I did to you, the person I cared most about in the world. I know I can't expect you to forgive me, but I'm asking anyway.'

'Of course I forgive you,' she said promptly. 'I understand how it must have looked. But you must know by now that it really was perfectly innocent, without question on my part, and I'm quite sure on Tony's as well.'

'That's what he says, too.'

'That last night I mentioned the one serious pass he did make, the first time he was at home, but that was before you and I had decided to get married.' She sighed. 'I don't know, maybe I should have told you about it then. If I had, maybe it

would have convinced you that I could never take
Tony seriously, not only because he's your brother,
but because of the kind of man he is, which certainly is the wrong kind of man for me.'

'Are you sure?' he asked carefully.

'Of course I'm sure!' she replied with an im-
patient gesture. 'It took me long enough to find
out. I thought you understood that.'

They sat there in silence for some time, each
wrapped in their own thoughts. Mark was staring
down at the floor, his arms crossed over his chest.
He looked terrible, his face drawn and gaunt, dark
circles under his eyes, lines across his forehead and
around his mouth that hadn't been there the last
time she'd seen him.

A sudden wave of tenderness for him swept over
her. She longed to go to him, put her arms around
him, tell him it would be all right. But she couldn't
do that. Even granted Tony deserved the beating,
still Mark somehow had to come to terms with his
own feelings, his own capacity for anger, his own
possessiveness.

Finally he raised his head. 'I guess there's not
much hope that you'd consider taking up where we
left off.'

'I don't know, Mark. You really frightened me
that night.'

'I'd never hurt you, Nora. I admit I wanted to
punish you when I thought you and Tony——' He
broke off and waved a hand in the air dismissively.
'But when it came right down to the wire, I couldn't
do it.'

Nora's mind raced. It was up to her. He was right,
after all. No matter how hurt and angry he'd been,

he had stopped himself from using his superior strength against her. Now here he was, humbling himself, a penitent asking her forgiveness. But there was a lot of pride in him, too. If she told him to go now, he'd leave without a murmur of protest. What was more, he'd stay away. She'd never see him again. Was that what she wanted?

On the other hand, if she continued the relationship, would she be attaching herself to another man who would break her heart? But Mark was not like the others. His jealousy might arise again one day, there was no guarantee it wouldn't. He was a possessive man who loved for keeps. But he would never lie to her, or trick her, or betray her.

Then, suddenly, it came to her in a blinding flash of insight that there was really only one important issue at stake. Did she love him? Watching him now, his good, honest face sunk in glum misery, she knew in her heart that, after the experience of loving and being loved by a man like Mark Leighton, all other men were spoiled for her forever.

'Mark?' she called softly to him.

He raised his head. 'Yes?'

'How long are you going to be in town?'

'As long as it takes,' was the prompt reply.

She smiled. 'All right, then, I'll tell you what. Today is Friday, and with this awful new job of mine I'm always dead beat by the end of the week.' She paused. 'And I still need a little time to think. Why don't you come over to my place some time tomorrow? I'll cook dinner for you.'

He gazed at her, his eyes alight, the old sparkle shining out of the liquid brown depths for the first time that day. 'All right,' he said with a warm, slow smile. 'I'll be there.'

At six-thirty the following evening, Nora sat at the window of her darkened living-room staring out at the street in front of the building. Every time a car swished by on the wet pavement below, she jumped to her feet, her heart pounding. But it was never Mark.

She'd been edgy all day, furious at herself for not giving him a specific time. In the morning she'd cleaned the apartment thoroughly and shopped for the steak dinner she planned to fix for him. After a late, meagre lunch at two o'clock of peanut-butter and crackers, she'd spent an hour getting bathed and dressed.

She'd wanted to wear something casual, yet flattering to her slim figure, and finally settled on the red woollen dress he had liked when she'd worn it before. Although it was a simple style with a low, square neck that buttoned decorously down the front, and was not really suggestive, it did fit her like a glove, and the colour was flattering to her pale complexion, sleek dark hair and green eyes.

In the small dining alcove the table was set for two, with her best cloth and the few pieces of good china she owned. She'd bought a small bunch of the first daffodils and placed them in a crystal vase in the centre, flanked by two tall yellow candles.

The steaks were marinating in the fridge, the potatoes all scrubbed and ready to pop into the oven, the salad greens washed and prepared. She'd been sitting there at the window since three o'clock watching and waiting, and still there was no sign of him.

By four o'clock, the pale morning sun had gradually become obscured by a bank of grey clouds, and a steady rain had begun to pour out of a leaden sky. By six it was growing dark, and, although she'd thought about turning on a lamp, by now she felt so dispirited that she didn't have the energy to move.

He wasn't coming. She'd just have to face it. But why hadn't he called to tell her? He was a man of his word. He'd said he'd be there, and that meant she could count on it.

She went into the kitchen to check on the steaks, then walked slowly back to her post by the window. What if he'd changed his mind? She hadn't exactly welcomed him with open arms when he'd shown up at her office yesterday. She could have been more encouraging.

After another half-hour of waiting, she was convinced it was hopeless. It was almost pitch-dark now, the rain still coming down. She got up and went over to switch on a lamp beside the couch, dragging her feet as she went. Then a terrible thought struck her. Maybe he'd had an accident! No, it couldn't be! The prospect of life without Mark didn't bear even thinking about.

Then, just as she turned on the lamp, she heard a car stop out in front. She ran back to the window and peered outside into the gloom. There he was, his familiar tall form silhouetted against the streetlight, just getting out of his car. She watched, her pulses racing, as he locked the car, then came sprinting towards the front entrance through the rain.

She ran to the door, running her fingers through her hair as she went, and flung it open to see him coming down the hall towards her, shrugging out of his wet trenchcoat on the way. He was dressed casually, tieless, in a pair of dark grey trousers, white shirt and navy jacket.

'I was beginning to get worried about you,' she called to him as he approached. It was an effort to keep her voice steady, to smile calmly, but to her relief she'd managed it.

'Sorry about that,' he said, shaking out his coat. 'I'd planned to come over earlier this afternoon, but one of my best mares decided to foal early, and I had to spend hours on the telephone with Ben talking him through the delivery.'

'Well, you're here now,' she said with a smile. 'That's all that matters. Come in and dry off.'

He stepped inside, and when she'd closed the door behind him she watched him while he hung his coat on the clothes-tree in the corner of the tiny entrance hall. He looked wonderful, tall and strong and as solid and reassuring as ever. There were still drops of rain sparkling on his black hair.

He turned around and started walking slowly towards her. Their eyes met and held until he stood before her. Then, wordlessly, he reached out and gathered her to him. She put her arms around his waist and buried her head in his shoulder with a deep sigh of relief. This was where she belonged. He was her strength.

He put a hand under her chin and tilted her head up to face him. His head came down, his mouth seeking hers in a long, slow kiss. After a while he lifted his head and drew back from her, his hands resting on her shoulders, his eyes boring into hers.

'Lord, how I love you, Nora,' he ground out in a shaky voice. 'I was terrified I'd lost you forever.' He gripped her shoulders a little harder. 'Do I dare hope you'll still marry me?'

The tenderness and love Nora saw shining out of the dark brown eyes gave her all the reassurance she needed. 'Yes, Mark,' she breathed. 'I'll marry you.'

His hold on her tightened, and he bent down to kiss her again, this time with more urgency. One hand slipped down from her shoulder to move back and forth across her breasts now, and she drew in a sharp breath as it slid underneath the opening of her dress to touch her bare flesh. She could hear her own shallow breathing, feel the ache of desire rising up in her as she gave herself up to the sensations his touch was arousing in her.

His mouth pressed more urgently against hers, opening wide as though to drink in her very soul. She felt his tongue on her lips, pressing, seeking entrance, then penetrating past them to fill the inside of her mouth. His feverish hand was clutching at her bare breast now, his thumb circling the taut peak.

'I can't wait,' he murmured against her lips. 'I want you so badly. I want you now.'

'Oh, yes, Mark,' she said. 'Yes, yes.'

Without another word, he swept her up in his arms and carried her down the hall to her bedroom. Inside he set her down beside the bed, then reached out and undid the top button of the red dress. His large hands moved downwards, pressing against her breasts as they went, until the last button was undone. Then slowly, carefully, he slipped the dress down over her shoulders and she stepped out of it.

She stood motionless, watching the gleam in his eyes grow brighter as his gaze travelled over her bare shoulders, the wispy flesh-coloured bra, the soft, rounded swell above it. Then, his eyes never leaving hers, he quickly shrugged out of his jacket and shirt and laid them beside her dress at the foot of the bed.

When he came back to her he reached out to run the tips of his fingers very lightly over the hard peaks of her breasts, back and forth, then in a slow, circular motion, until the ache became unbearable.

'Oh, Mark,' she choked out, her eyes pleading.

He smiled and undid the front clasp of her bra. As he pulled the straps down over her arms, his fingertips brushing lightly over the naked, burning flesh, she closed her eyes and let her head fall back, lost in an agony of longing.

'You're so beautiful, darling,' he murmured.

She leaned forward slightly so that her full breasts filled his waiting hands, then felt his moist lips close over one hard nipple, his softly rasping tongue bathing it gently. She put her hands on his dark head, pressing it closely against her breast.

Finally, she couldn't bear the sweet torment a moment longer. She opened her eyes and reached out to run her own hands down that strong, beautiful body, from his broad shoulders, over his smooth, muscular chest, his flat stomach until they reached the waistband of his trousers. His muscles and sinews rippled under her touch, and he, too, was trembling.

He reached down, swiftly undid the trousers and stepped out of them. Then he knelt before her and slid off the last scrap of her underwear. As he rose slowly to his feet, his hands and mouth left a path of fire along her entire body, until they stood facing each other again, heart to pounding heart.

He eased her down backwards on the bed and lowered himself gently on top of her, his hard, pulsing masculinity thrusting against her, his hot skin burning on hers, until finally she could bear it no longer and she cried out, 'Now, Mark! Oh, please, now!'

'Oh, yes, darling,' she heard him groan, and they were joined together at last.

As they rode the crest of the wave together into an ecstatic climax, Nora clung to the man she loved, tumbling headlong over the precipice with him. And, as she slowly wafted down from the heights in Mark's arms, she knew that she was free of the wrong kind of man forever.

HARLEQUIN
Romance

Coming Next Month

FREE GIFT OFFER

To receive your free gift, send us the specified number of proofs-of-purchase from any specially marked Free Gift Offer Harlequin or Silhouette book with the Free Gift Certificate properly completed, plus a check or money order (do not send cash) to cover postage and handling payable to Harlequin/Silhouette Free Gift Promotion Offer. We will send you the specified gift.

FREE GIFT CERTIFICATE

ITEM	A. GOLD TONE EARRINGS	B. GOLD TONE BRACELET	C. GOLD TONE NECKLACE
# of proofs-of-purchase required	3	6	9
Postage and Handling	$1.75	$2.25	$2.75
Check one	☐	☐	☐

Name: _____

Address: _____

City: _____ State: _____ Zip Code: _____

Mail this certificate, specified number of proofs-of-purchase and a check or money order for postage and handling to: HARLEQUIN/SILHOUETTE FREE GIFT OFFER 1992, P.O. Box 9057, Buffalo, NY 14269-9057. Requests must be received by July 31, 1992.

PLUS—Every time you submit a completed certificate with the correct number of proofs-of-purchase, you are automatically entered in our MILLION DOLLAR SWEEPSTAKES! No purchase or obligation necessary to enter. See below for alternate means of entry and how to obtain complete sweepstakes rules.

MILLION DOLLAR SWEEPSTAKES
NO PURCHASE OR OBLIGATION NECESSARY TO ENTER

To enter, hand-print (mechanical reproductions are not acceptable) your name and address on a 3"×5" card and mail to Million Dollar Sweepstakes 6097, c/o either P.O. Box 9056, Buffalo, NY 14269-9056 or P.O. Box 621, Fort Erie, Ontario L2A 5X3. Limit: one entry per envelope. Entries must be sent via 1st-class mail. For eligibility, entries must be received no later than March 31, 1994. No liability is assumed for printing errors, lost, late or misdirected entries.

Sweepstakes is open to persons 18 years of age or older. All applicable laws and regulations apply. Sweepstakes offer void wherever prohibited by law. Prizewinners will be determined no later than May 1994. Chances of winning are determined by the number of entries distributed and received. For a copy of the Official Rules governing this sweepstakes offer, send a self-addressed, stamped envelope (WA residents need not affix return postage) to: Million Dollar Sweepstakes Rules, P.O. Box 4733, Blair, NE 68009.

✂ HR2U

ONE PROOF-OF-PURCHASE
To collect your fabulous FREE GIFT you must include the necessary FREE GIFT proofs-of-purchase with a properly completed offer certificate.

(See inside back cover for offer details)